Black Barbie

by
Comfort Arthur

—

for
Afia Safowaa

One day, my mother bought me a *Black Barbie.*

"I don't like it!" I groaned.

"I WANT THE WHITE ONE!"

I moaned.

I grabbed it and stormed away—
an impolite display,
much to my mum's dismay.

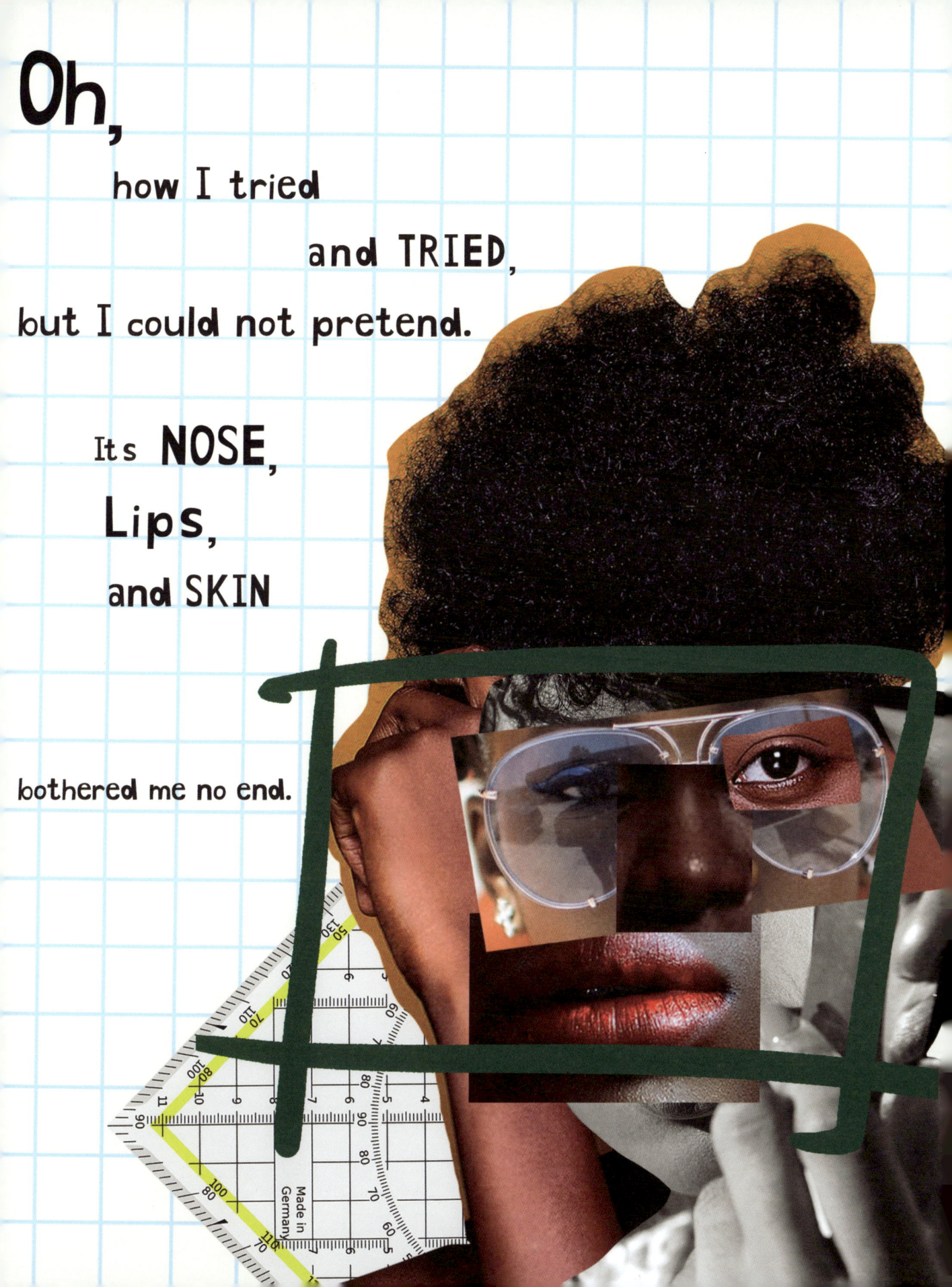

Oh,
how I tried
 and TRIED,
but I could not pretend.

Its **NOSE**,
Lips,
and **SKIN**

bothered me no end.

My black doll's flesh felt **HARD**
and **COLD,**

uncomfortable to *touch*

and

HOLD.

Sometimes I would

SQUEEZE her tight,

but push her away in **MORNING** light.

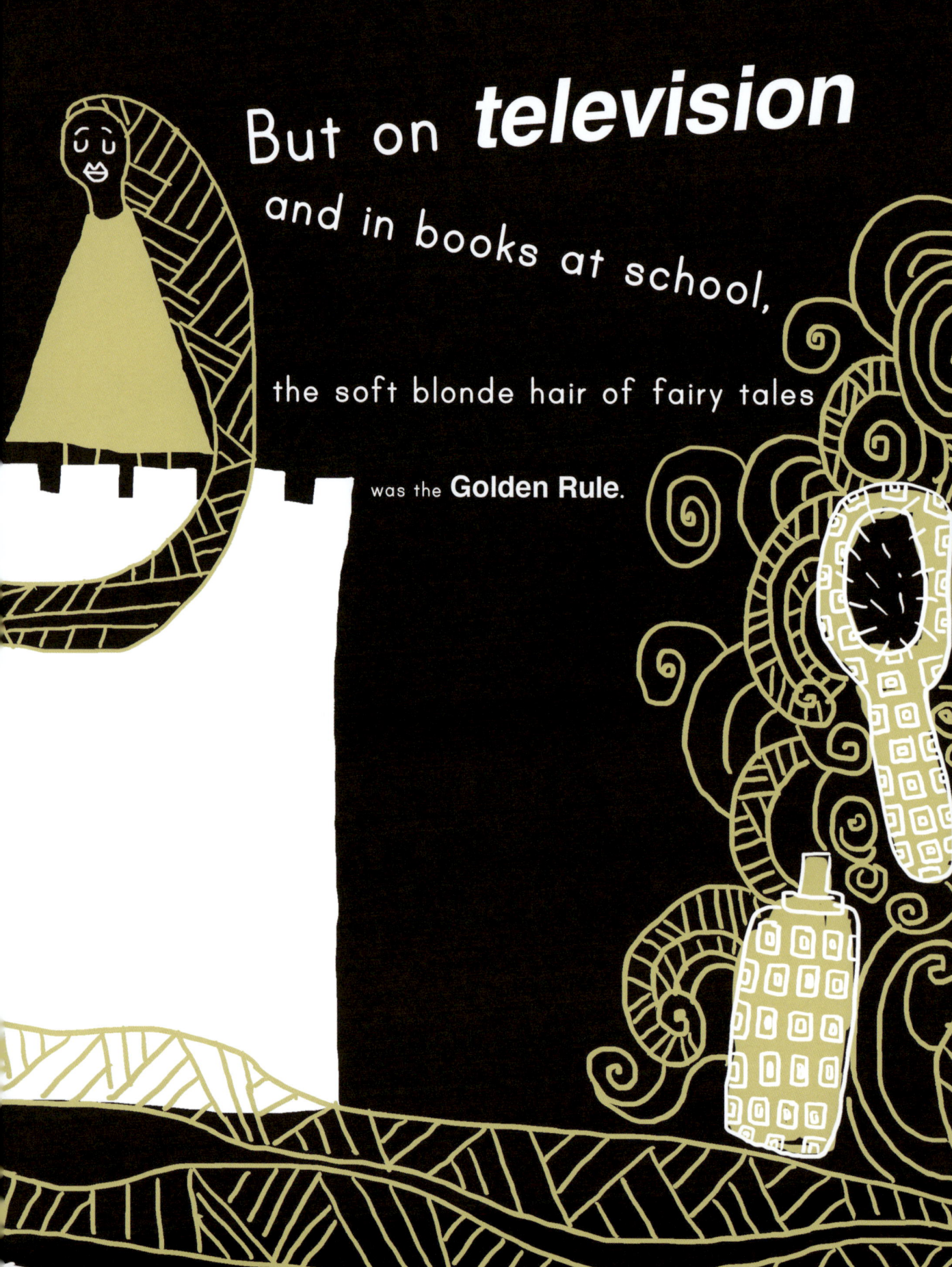

So, when I was twenty-three, at the beauty counter, one fateful day I had my first bleaching cream encounter.

"Will this work for me?" I asked, my eyes wide and frightened. "Yes," the man said cheerfully, "your tone will be enlightened."

Rubbing it into my skin, the smell made me recoil. Chemicals burned my flesh and felt like flaming oil.

That night, in the mirror, I painfully recalled my disdain for **Black Barbie** and I was appalled. When I'd left my black doll unloved on the shelf, I'd failed to see the beauty that flowered in myself.

and have my kind of hair.

I WISH I HAD THIS BOOK WHEN I WAS YOUNGER.

As a young Black girl I often pondered: Am I pretty enough? Light enough? Thin enough? Smart enough? Over the years, this frustration built up until, as an adult, I proclaimed, "Enough is enough!"

This powerful book reminds every young Black woman that you are more than enough. You are the standard of beauty, with your glowing melanin skin, the intricacy of your precious locks, and the vibrance of Black Girl Magic that fills every room that you enter.

Young girls look to their dolls as a source of inspiration and reassurance. Unfortunately, when the vast majority of dolls on the shelf at the store are blonde, blue-eyed, and feature the same distorted, uniform body size, this is often an empty, even futile pursuit. The harmfulness of this singular representation was made crystal clear during the legendary U.S. Supreme Court case, Brown v. Board of Education, which effectively paved the way for ending racial segregation in U.S. public schools.

The plaintiffs, led by future Supreme Court Justice Thurgood Marshall, cited a doll test known as the "Clark Test," where Black children were asked basic questions about the intellectual capacity and worth of Black dolls versus White dolls. Tragically, the overwhelming majority characterized Blackness as 'looking bad' and not a 'nice color.'

Sixty-six years later, we still grapple with the negative associations of Blackness and identity. As we look deeper, we find the beauty within and unveil the limitless potential of each Black girl. Thank you, Comfort Arthur, for guiding us on this journey of discovery and hope, beauty, and the love of our culture, prompting us to stand and proclaim in unison: "Black is Beautiful."

This book captures the essence of identity, beauty, and purpose. It delves into the depth of one's inner soul and wraps you in the embrace of unconditional love.

Dr. Artika R. Tyner is an author and the founding director of the Center on Race, Leadership and Social Justice, and an alumni of University of St. Thomas School of Law. She is deeply committed to teaching students of all ages how to create new structures for equity and inclusion, social justice and freedom. She is the recipient of more than two dozen awards, including: American Bar Association Difference Makers; Women in Business; American Small Business Champion; and International Educator Citizen. Dr. Tyner is also the founder of Planting People, Growing Justice Leadership Institute, an organization committed to promoting literacy and diversity in books. You can learn more about her work at: www.artikatyner.com.

TOOLS FOR PARENTS AND CAREGIVERS

• Create daily positive affirmations to remind Black girls everywhere that they are beautiful, inside and out. Start by creating 3 powerful "I am" statements, such as: I am strong. I am smart. I am beautiful.

• Post and hang images that depict the beauty and magnificence of women of women of African descent. Start with the matriarch of your family and share her story of triumph. Hang artwork from African artists, portraits of historical Black female icons and contemporary Black women role models in all walks of life.

• Invest in reading materials specifically created for the young women in your life. These books will serve as a source of inspiration and guidance while encouraging her to discover the leader within.

Black Barbie copyright 2020 by Comfort Arthur.
All rights reserved. No part of this book may be reproduced in any form whatsoever, by photography or xerography or by any other means, by broadcast or transmission, by
translation into any kind of languge, nor by recording electronically or otherwise, without permission in writing from the author, except by a reviewer, who may quote brief passages in citable articles or reviews.

ISBN: 978-1-64343-851-1
Printed in the United States of America
First Printing: 2020
25 24 23 22 21   5 4 3 2 1
Edited by Lily Coyle and John Schaidler
Print preparation by Becca Hart

Beaver's Pond Press
939 Seventh Street West
Saint Paul, Minnesota 55102
(952) 829-8818
www.BeaversPondPress.com
To order, visit TheComfyStudio.com/BlackBarbie
Reseller discounts available.

A Golden Treasury

Victoria and Albert Musuem • Indian Art Series

Victoria and Albert Museum • Indian Art Series

A Golden Treasury
Jewellery from the Indian Subcontinent

Susan Stronge, Nima Smith and J.C. Harle

Victoria and Albert Museum
in association with
Mapin Publishing Pvt. Ltd.

Reprinted 1995

This book accompanies an exhibition
at Cartwright Hall, Bradford Art Galleries
and Museums, Lister Park, Bradford, from
24 September-27 November 1988
and at Zamana Gallery, London, from
13 April-25 June 1989.

First published in the United States of America
by Grantha Corporation, Middletown, NJ 07701

Simultaneously published by the
Victoria and Albert Museum, London
in association with
Mapin Publishing Pvt. Ltd, Ahmedabad
by arrangement with
Grantha Corporation
80 Cliffedgeway, Middletown, NJ 07701

Text copyright © 1988, 1995 Susan Stronge, Nima Smith,
and J.C. Harle
Illustrations copyright © as listed, 1988, 1995

All rights reserved.
No part of this publication may be reproduced,
stored in a retrieval system, or transmitted,
in any form or by any means, electronic,
mechanical, photocopying, recording or otherwise,
without the prior written permission of the publisher.

ISBN 0-9441-4216-8 (Grantha)
ISBN 81-85822-26-3 (Mapin)
LC 88-50857

Distributors:
India & Nepal:
The Variety Book Depot
AVG Bhawan, M-3 Connaught Circus,
New Delhi 110001

UK and Europe:
Gazelle Book Services, Lancaster

Asia:
Mapin Publishing Pvt. Ltd., Ahmedabad.

Series editor: John Guy
Editor: Susan Stronge
Editorial consultant: Carmen Kagal
Editorial assistant: Graham Parlett
Designer: Yvonne Dedman

Typeset in Linotron Bembo
by Fotocomp Systems, Bombay
Printed and bound by
Mandarin Offset, Hong Kong

Indian Art Series colophon (p.1): Lakshmi, the Hindu
goddess of good fortune and the embodiment of
grace and charm, standing on a lotus above the
sacred ocean from which she was born. The goddess
is freuently worshipped in the home and the
temple to bring good luck and to avert misfortune.
Impression of a copper seal with a Gaja-Lakshmi
design, North India; c.6th-7th century.

Endpapers: Design based on a detail from an armlet
(no. 86)

Frontispiece: Hair ornament (no. 51)

Contents

Acknowledgments   7

Jewellery in Indian Sculpture · 11

Dr James Harle
Formerly Keeper of Eastern Art
Ashmolean Museum

Ancient Jewellery   16
Gold Coins   24

Jewellery of the Mughal Period · 27

Susan Stronge
Victoria and Albert Museum

The Treasury of the World   27
The South   38
India and the West   43
Tribal Jewellery   47

Turban Jewels   51
Ornaments for the Head   57
Pendants and Necklaces   68
Arm Ornaments   88
Rings   94
Anklets   98
Jewellery made for Europeans   100
Miscellany   108
Naga Jewellery   111

The Darker Side of Gold · 115

Dr Nima Smith
Bradford Art Galleries and Museums

Twentieth-century Jewellery   124

Glossary   138

Bibliography   140

Index   142

Acknowledgments

All objects in the catalogue are from the collection of the Victoria and Albert Museum, except where stated in the entries. We are enormously indebted to the lenders:

Her Majesty the Queen
The Ashmolean Museum, Oxford
The British Museum, London
The Pitt Rivers Museum, Oxford
Dr D.H. Calam
Mr Christopher R. Cavey, FGS
Mrs Sheila Horsbrugh

Without Julie Sadler's secretarial help the catalogue would probably never have been finished; Hugh Sainsbury heroically worked through the enormous task of photography; in the Indian Department of the Victoria and Albert Museum, Robert Skelton and colleagues were always available for assistance and advice; Mr Joe Cribb of the British Museum catalogued the coins and Dr Roger Harding of the British Museum (Natural History) examined a great many of the gemstones.

We are particularly grateful to the following organisations for their financial assistance:

The Arts Council of Great Britain, Bradford Economic Development Unit, the Crafts Council, Shell UK Ltd, the Yorkshire Arts Association and the Zamana Gallery.

In addition, we gratefully acknowledge the individuals and organisations who have helped in many different ways:

Mr Ralph Turner's enthusiasm was greatly appreciated in the initial planning of the exhibition; Miss Vivienne Becker and Mrs Shirley Bury gave indispensable guidance concerning the jewellery made in the European taste; Mr Andrew Topsfield and Mr Arthur MacGregor of the Ashmolean Museum; Dr Robert Knox, Dr Michael Rogers, Miss Venetia Porter and Mr Richard Blurton of the British Museum; Dr Schuyler Jones and Mrs Valerie Mowet of the Pitt Rivers Museum; Mr Ronald Lightbown and Mr Richard Edgcumbe of the Victoria and Albert Museum; Dr Rupert Snell, Dr A. S. Melikian–Chirvani and Mr A. A. Tavakkoli for their linguistic help; Mr P. L. R. Smith; Mr P. G. Isaacs; Mr R. Parmar; Prof. P. Lall and Tribhovandas Bhimji Zaveri.

Illustration Acknowledgments
All illustrations are the copyright of the Victoria and Albert Museum, with the following exceptions:

The Ashmolean Museum, Oxford: figs. 2, 4, 12; nos. 80, 82, 104
BBC Hulton Picture Library: fig. 23
The British Museum, London: fig. 8; nos. 16–25, 27–36, 63, 81, 97, 101, 102
Camera Crew, Bradford: nos. 130–71
The Cleveland Museum of Art: fig. 3
A.C. Cooper: nos. 42, 77, 121
Gemäldegalerie, Staatliche Museen Preussischer Kulturbesitz, Berlin (West): fig. 18
The Metropolitan Museum of Art, New York: fig. 1
The Pitt Rivers Museum, Oxford: nos. 60, 126–9. (photographed by Malcolm Osman)
Robert Harding Picture Library: figs. 24, 25
The Royal Anthropological Institute, London: fig. 20
The Royal Institute of British Architects, London: fig. 15
Studio Colophon, Leicester: fig. 22

Abbreviations

BM   British Museum
V&A   Victoria and Albert Museum
AH   *Anno hegirae* (the Islamic calendar)
VS   *Vikrama Samvat* (one of the Hindu
        calendar systems)
H   Height
L   Length
W   Width
D   Depth
DIAM.   Diameter

All measurements exclude thread ties and small pendant stones.

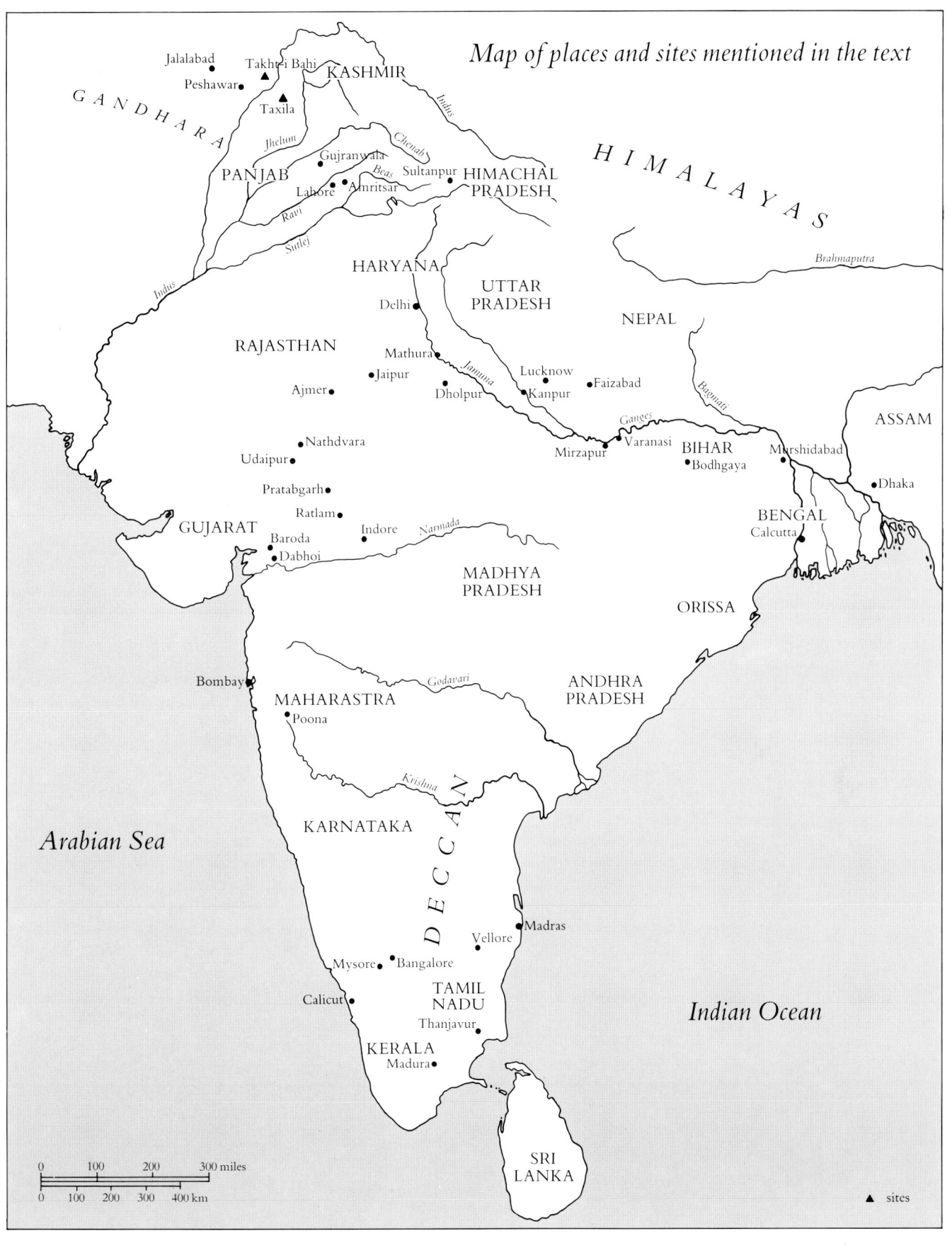

Jewellery in Indian Sculpture

Gold has been highly valued since earliest times because of its inalterability and its adaptability to all sorts of uses. It is the only metal found in a usable form in its natural state. Of all the metals known, until very recently, it is the most valuable. Gold coins, when they are minted (rather rarely in historical terms) stand at the head of every coinage.

Gold has been found practically everywhere in the world, even in seawater, but in vastly varying quantities. It very often contains an admixture of silver in its natural state. In early times it was gathered from river beds or from shale deposits on hillsides, requiring no more technology than a pick of some sorts and a pan. It is relatively rare in the Indian subcontinent, although Nepal has considerable deposits. Most of the gold in India proper is found in Karnataka and today it is mined industrially in the Kolar gold fields. Most of the gold in India, however, is imported and was even in ancient times. India has an insatiable appetite for gold. Almost all of it is in private hands, widely distributed even into the villages, as compared to many other countries where it is principally held by their Central Banks as an element of their financial role. This is because it remains, in the form of jewellery, the principal, indeed practically the only form of wealth available to the women of India, and as such is an important part of the dowry system.

In India, gold has had many uses. The gold coins of the Guptas, from an artistic point of view, are amongst the finest ever minted. Completely new is the practice of portraying royal pursuits and accomplishments on some of the coins, for example, the rhinoceros hunt or the king playing a stringed instrument. The Mughals also minted splendidly in gold. The finest enamels in India had a gold base. Gold, as elsewhere, has always been extensively used for rings and other mountings of gems.

Images of gold are mentioned in the texts and by the Chinese pilgrims but none of any size have survived. Any large golden object is in constant danger of being melted down. The very finest of the reliquaries deposited in stupas were, like the Bimaran reliquary in the British Museum, of gold; inside the simpler stone ones, the little containers which held the relics were then of gold. Gilding of images was common, particularly in Nepal, where gold was plentiful, and also in Tibet. Gold was also used in alloys, according to ritual prescriptions.

It was in jewellery and ornament, however, that gold seems to have been most regularly employed. The Vedic gods are constantly described as wearing ornaments made of gold. Small pieces of gold jewellery are common but not plentiful at Harappan sites. Throughout their long history until the present day, the Indian peoples seem always to have been particularly fond of adornment. This is true of many other peoples, but not all: the ancient Egyptians, whose craftsmanship was certainly the equal of that of the ancient Indians, used it sparingly, if the figures portrayed on their sculptures and their reliefs are any indication. Most Indian

Fig. 1
A *yakshi*.
Moulded terracotta plaque
Tamluk, the ancient Tamralipti,
c. 200 BC
Ashmolean Museum: X201

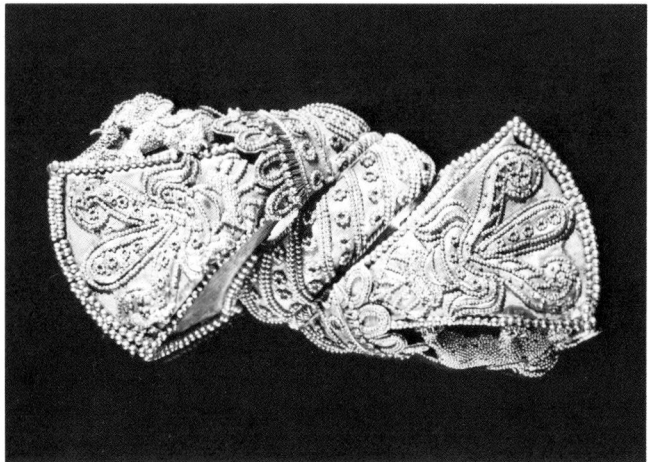 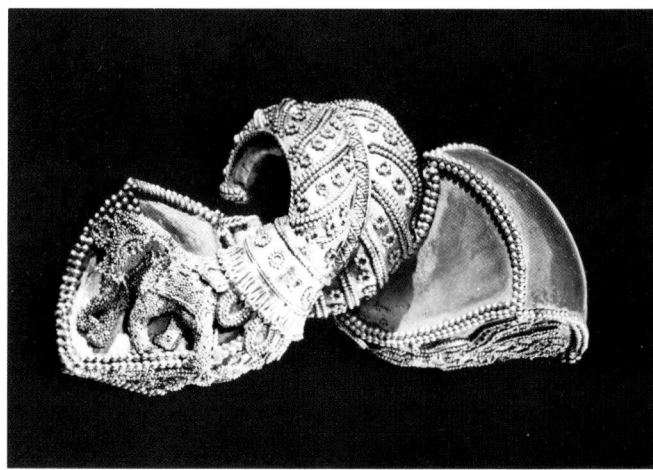

Fig. 2
One of a pair of royal earrings
Granulated gold
India, perhaps Andhra Pradesh;
c. 1st century BC
Metropolitan Museum of Art,
New York: 1981.398.3
Gift of the Kronos Collections,
1981

jewellery was of silver or base metals; even terracotta has been pressed into service since Harappan times, as earrings and bangles from excavated sites of all periods show. In the same way, plastic bangles are prevalent today; lest they be totally disparaged, one should remember that they are the successors to a long tradition of glass and lac bangles. Certain groups of women, notably Marwaris, may even today be seen loaded down with silver jewellery; amongst certain women of the scheduled castes, base metal jewellery is worn in profusion, often preserving traditional types, since it is not worth melting down. Gold jewellery, often set with precious or semi-precious stones, is worn more discreetly. Except in princely circles and on certain occasions such as weddings the wearing of large amounts of jewellery appears, for several centuries now, to have been the prerogative of women. At first glance it may appear that this was not the case in ancient India since sculpture is replete with richly adorned male figures. One must remember, however, that practically all of these represent gods, and their costumes and adornments were undoubtedly modelled on those of the royalty and nobility of the day.

Striking evidence of this is provided by the Kronos earrings in the Metropolitan Museum of Art, without question the finest pieces of early Indian jewellery known to date (fig. 2).[1] Their find-place is not known but it has been pointed out that very similar earrings are worn by the Chakravartin (World Emperor) on the famous relief from Jaggayyapeta in eastern Andhra (c. first century BC).[2] Herein perhaps lies the clue to why practically none of the bulky jewellery depicted in the stone sculpture has survived. The connection here between these massive earrings and royalty (the lion and the elephant are royal beasts) suggests that few such sumptuous pieces were ever made. What we know of ancient Indian jewellery is derived from two sources: excavated material from early sites with gold jewellery relatively rare, and the visual record provided by countless carved or, more rarely, painted, representations of richly adorned gods and goddesses from the third to fourth centuries BC onwards. The two do not always correspond very closely. Representations of jewellery tend to be more massive and very little of this sort was probably made in the first place. The techniques of carving stone or moulding terracottas, moreover, do not favour the reproduction of lighter, more delicate creations such as have been found in excavations in the north-west; the jewellery shown in the Ajanta murals is more akin to them, at least in spirit. Finally, there is an ever increasing tendency, commencing in the later part of the Gupta period (c. 500 AD), for the jewellery worn by stone or bronze figures to become conventionalised and no longer represent real jewellery. This development, like so many others, does not appear until much later in Tamilnadu.

Of the relatively rare finds of ancient gold jewellery, most are from the north-west of the subcontinent, the region known as Gandhara in ancient times, and particularly from Taxila, a flourishing city since at least the fourth century BC and which has been extensively excavated. As one would expect, most of this jewellery shows a strong Greek or Hellenistic influence. Earrings (nos. 3–6) often consist of discs from which hang down tiny chains terminating in beads or sometimes small gold erotes, or cupids, in repoussé. Such pendants also hang down over almost their whole length from necklaces when they are of the 'strap' variety. Ribbing is practised, sometimes for the terminal elements of necklaces, but spherical ribbed beads, found in considerable numbers, appear to be an Indian type. A pair of heavy round tubular bracelets of a purely Indian type were also found at Taxila, of the type worn by the *yakshi* from Tamluk (fig. 1).

Of the early sculpture figures which have survived, none wears as much or as sumptuous jewellery as this *yakshi* on a moulded terracotta plaque found at Tamluk near Calcutta, of c.200 BC. It is interesting to note examples of practically every type of jewellery so far found in excavations. These include the strings of beads dangling from her girdle and below; the former even have pendants in the form of small squatting figures. From the discs at the ends of her massive earrings hang, fringe-like, small strings of beads, and part of her girdle is composed of round ribbed beads. The long pins stuck into her headdress are headed, not by figures (see no. 16) but by auspicious symbols, such as the trident and the elephant goad. The most intricate piece of jewellery depicted, however, hardly visible to the naked eye, is the clasp to the bandolier across the goddess's chest composed of a deer and a *makara* (a semi-aquatic mythical beast which plays an important part in Indian iconography). It is quite likely that in the real thing they would have been covered with granulation.

The characteristic sculpture of Gandhara during the first three or four centuries AD was produced, in vast quantities, for the Buddhists and their monasteries (fig. 3). Consequently, with the notable exception of Hariti (see nos. 1 and 26), the figures with adornments are all masculine Bodhisattvas, decked in the finery of a local magnate (the Buddha, of course, wears no jewellery of any kind until much later). These favoured massive earrings, armlets and torques, often incorporating bird or animal forms. On their diadems and armlets can sometimes be seen the high-haunched animals of the 'Animal Style'. Only one or two examples, possibly imports, of the Sarmatian and Scythian jewellery from Southern Russia have been found in India.[3] On the other hand, there are examples (no. 17) of the tubular reliquaries almost invariably strung along the *yajnopavitas* (sacred thread) of the Bodhisattvas.

Just after the Gupta period (320 AD–c. 550 AD), the jewellery portrayed on statues becomes increasingly conventionalised and removed from the actual practice

Fig. 3
Bodhisattva
Grey schist
Gandhara; Kushana period, late 2nd century AD
The Cleveland Museum of Art, purchase from the J.H. Wade Fund
65.476

14 · Jewellery in Indian Sculpture

Fig. 4
The 'Hedges' Vishnu
Ceriticised slate (siltstone)
Sagar Island, West Bengal;
c. 1050
Ashmolean Museum: AM 169

of the goldsmiths (fig. 4); so is the vocabulary used to describe the various pieces of jewellery: necklace (*hāra*), armlet (*keyurā*), bracelet (*kaṅkana*), earring (*kuṇḍala*), girdle (*mekhalā*) and so on. These Sanskrit names, taken from the classical and traditional literature, had been replaced, in the parlance of the goldsmith, his clients and patrons, by terms in the vernacular languages, and remained the province only of the ritualist, the iconographer and the student of literature. The general nature and position of these adornments, and even some motifs, are on the whole pan-Indian: a pipal leaf at the end of a chain (see no. 25) may be seen depicted on a Pala relief from Eastern India of the tenth century[4] and on Chola bronzes of approximately the same date. At the same time – and this may appear paradoxical – as the regional styles of sculpture develop and diverge, the jewellery depicted takes on some of their characteristics: that of the Hoysala style appears somewhat frilly, that of the Chandellas, at Khajuraho, for example, over-simplified and tending to the linear.

Footnotes

1. Lerner, 1984, pp. 20 and 21
2. This is in the Government Museum, Madras. See H. Zimmer, *The Art of Indian Asia*, New York, 1955, rd. 2, pl. 37.
3. See M.I. Rostovtseff, *Animal Style in South Russia and China*, Princeton, 1929, pl. XVIII, 5.
4. Stele of Kamadeva, Patna Museum (6046). For publication, see Bautze-Picron (cf. no. 24).

Ancient Jewellery

1
Plaque with Hariti and Panchika (Kubera)
Gold repoussé
Taxila(?), Panjab; Kushana period, 1st–2nd century AD
W 4.4 cm H 3.6 cm
IS 10-1948
Formerly collection Col. D.H. Gordon

The god and goddess are depicted seated side by side surrounded by a beaded border. Hariti was an ancient folk goddess, the purloiner and then protectress of children, and was associated with smallpox. Her consort Panchika (or Kubera) was a folk god associated with wealth and was the guardian of one of the four quarters. Both were adopted into the Buddhist pantheon, innumerable portrayals of them being made in stone showing them seated together. This depiction was no doubt partly influenced by similar Roman tutelary couples, almost invariably in 'foreign' dress, hers Hellenistic, his most often that of the Kushanas. Here, he holds a staff in his left hand, she a flower: what their right hands held, if anything, cannot be discerned.

An exceptional feature of this pair is that they are shown, as nowhere else, with the goddess on Panchika's proper right, instead of left. This is so extraordinary as to suggest that the maker of the die had forgotten to reverse the position of his figures so that they would appear in the correct order when hammered out on a sheet of gold. A somewhat similar gold plaque, but with the figures wearing Indian costume, appears among the contents of a gilded schist reliquary (Czuma, 1985, pp. 166A and 167).

PUBLISHED
Ashton (ed.), 1947-8, no. 192 p. 156.
Doshi (ed.), 1985, p. v.

2 *(see p. 20)*
Goddess holding a mirror
Gold, lac-filled base
Taxila(?), Panjab; 2nd century BC–1st century AD
H 5 cm DIAM. of base 2 cm
IS 13-1948

The little figure of the goddess is entirely Hellenistic in pose and dress; only the Indian-style lotus base indicates that she is not an import. While statues of Aphrodite, the Roman Venus, are legion in the west from Greek and Hellenistic times to the Roman period, there seem to be few if any exact models for this figure, standing fully clothed and holding a mirror in her left hand (Salomon Reinach, *Répertoire de la Statuaire Grecque et Romaine*, 6 vols., Paris, 1913–14). These miniature figures of the goddess of love were frequently used as pin finials (Herbert Hoffmann and Patricia F. Davidson, 1965–6, p. 192, figs. 72a and b; Reynold Higgins, 1980, pl. 53g); and cf. no. 16.

PUBLISHED
H. Buchtal, 'The Haughton Collection of Gandhara Sculpture', *The Burlington Magazine*, LXXXVI, 1945, p. 66, pl. IA.

Catalogue nos. 2–14 were formerly in the collection of Major-General H. L. Haughton, brought together from the Panjab and the North West Frontier Province.

3
Earring
Gold
Taxila(?), Panjab; 1st–2nd century AD(?)
H 4.4 cm
IS 16-1948

The earring consists of a six-petalled blossom with a circular centre of applied wire enclosed by granules of regular size. The inner petals, cut from sheet gold, are plain; the outer petals, of stamped sheet gold, are filled with granules of differing sizes. Twisted wires are attached to the back and appear as loops from the front, adorned with granulated rosettes. Beneath the blossom is a turquoise vase mounted with granulated sheet gold; linking the vase and rosette are stylised dolphins of sheet gold. Miniature vases are common in Greek and Hellenistic jewellery. The find-place, simply given as Taxila, begs the question of which site it came from, vitally important in assigning a date to these four earrings. The most likely site would appear to be Sirkap, the first-century BC–first-century AD city (see John Marshall, 1951).

4
Earring
Gold
Taxila(?), Panjab; 1st–2nd century AD
H 4.1 cm
IS 19-1948

This, like the preceding earring, has a vase pendant, here made of a pearl with finely granulated gold mounts, and with a pedestal foot. The dolphins are more naturalistic, worked in the round and chased. A trefoil of sheet gold, with applied wire and granulated borders, replaces the blossom. Three seed pearls are attached by chains to the top of the earring.

5
Earring
Gold
Taxila(?), Panjab; 1st–2nd century AD(?)
H 4.3 cm
IS 18-1948

This earring has a blossom with five heart-shaped petals, filled with granulation, their points meeting at a small central disc. The pendant beneath has a compressed spherical bead, a ring of granules, and a turquoise bead set in gold and with a granulated terminal. The twisted wire loops seen on no. 3, set with granulated rosettes, are repeated here.

6
Earring
Gold
Taxila(?), Panjab; 1st-2nd century AD(?)
H 3.5 cm
IS 17-1948

The blossom is of the same type as no. 3 and has the same twisted wire loops. Beneath is a leaf, or stylised butterfly, of sheet gold with two vertical rows of granules. An earring with a similar blossom and the same characteristic applied twisted wires is illustrated by Brunel, 1972, fig. 9. Although he calls it Gupta and dates it to the fifth century, it would seem to be from the same workshop that made this earring and no. 3.

3
4 6
5

18 · *Jewellery in Indian Sculpture*

7
Bead in the shape of an elephant
Potstone
North-west of Indian subcontinent; 2nd century BC–2nd century AD
W 1.5 cm H 1.4 cm
IS 26-1948

The pierced bead has a human figure of indeterminate sex incised on the base.

8
Bead in the shape of a mango
Lilac and golden brown agate, pierced
North-west of Indian subcontinent; 2nd century BC–2nd century AD
H 2.6 cm W 2.1 cm
IS 27-1948

9
Bead in the shape of a bird
Almandine garnet
Taxila(?), North-west Frontier Province; c. 1st century BC
H 1.2 cm
IS 28-1948

A similar example, also with its head broken off, was published by Horace C. Beck, 'The Beads from Taxila', *Memoirs of the Archaeological Survey of India,* no. 65, 1941, pl. VII 17, as coming from the Dharmarajika *stupa* at Taxila.

7

8

9

10
Seal
Greenish-grey chalcedony; engraved with a griffin
North-west of Indian subcontinent; 2nd century BC–2nd century AD
H 1.5 cm W 2 cm D 1 cm
IS 32-1948

The seal has longitudinal piercing parallel to the body of the griffin. It is domed, with chamfered sides, and was probably set on a swivel in a pendant or a ring. A griffin is a mythical animal of Greek and Roman art, usually depicted with a lion's legs and body, wings, and an eagle's head. Here the wings, head and tail are those of a griffin, but the body and legs are those of a horse. The rounded forms of the body belong to Iranian tradition.

11
Seal
Bloodstone; engraved with a sitting bull
North-west of Indian subcontinent(?)
2nd century BC–2nd century AD
DIAM. of flat face 1.4 cm
IS 36-1948

This seal consists of three-quarters of a sphere and is pierced through the centre. The bull is the humped Indian bull *(Bos indicus)*. The rounded forms, as in no. 10, attest to Iranian tradition, here reinforced by the shape of the seal which is typical of Iranian examples.

12
Seal
Carnelian; engraved with a winged horse
North-west of Indian subcontinent, but possibly an import from the West; 2nd century BC–2nd century AD
H 1.6 cm W 1.7 cm D 0.4 cm
IS 39-1948

This seal is flat on front and back. It is of extremely fine workmanship, and from its technique might be the work of a Greek engraver. While the flying horse strikes a familar note as Pegasus, representations of the winged horse are not common on Greek and Roman seals.

11 12 10
13 (seal) 13 (impression) 14

Ancient Jewellery · 19

13
Seal
Crystal, Hercules subduing the Nemean lion
North-west of Indian subcontinent; Gupta period (320–550 AD)
H 2.7 cm W 1.8 cm
IS 43-1948

This fine seal, displaying a masterly technique which might presuppose a Greek engraver and done in a western classical style, is nonetheless apparently an original iconographic rendering which suggests an eastern origin. One of the twelve labours of Hercules, his combat with the Nemean lion has been depicted innumerable times in Hellenistic and Roman sculpture. But the iconographic formula of Hercules holding the upright lion in a stranglehold around the neck (an example of which, carved in the local stone and of Kushana date, was found in Mathura) is quite different from the combat depicted here. The seal has a Gupta-period inscription: *Srīctasaya* or *sricetasya*.

14
Seal
Sardonyx, depicting Hariti(?)
North-west of Indian subcontinent; c. 2nd–4th century AD
H 2.5 cm W 1.9 cm D 0.3 cm
IS 46-1948

While not cut to the highest standard, this seal is an excellent example of a western classical style and technique adapting itself to Indian costume and iconography. This goddess is probably Hariti, wearing obviously Indian dress in contrast to her clothing in nos. 1 and 26. The cornucopia she holds in her left hand shows no understanding of its Greek or Roman model; the sword in her right hand is not one of Hariti's attributes and suggests that the seal was produced in the same Indo-Iranian religious climate that produced the divinities on the reverse of Kushana coins (see no. 27).

15
Relic container
Gold
Takht-i Bahi, North-west Frontier Province; 2nd–5th century AD
H 3 cm DIAM. 2.4 cm
IS 229b-1951

Small gold boxes, usually cylindrical, were often placed in stone reliquaries as containers for the actual relics, in this case bone fragments and two small beads (see Stanislas J. Czuma, 1985, pp.165–7, for illustrations of a superb stone reliquary and its contents, including several little gold boxes). Takht-i Bahi, by the road to the Malakand Pass and Swat, is one of the best preserved Buddhist monasteries in what was Gandhara.

2 15

20 · *Jewellery in Indian Sculpture*

16
Hair-pin finial in the form of a goddess
Gold
Gandhara; 1st–2nd century AD(?)
H 5 cm
BM: 1962.11-12.1
Brookes-Sewell Bequest

Unlike no. 2, the goddess here is semi-nude and entirely western classical in style. Her left hand, held up close to her shoulder, holds a small stick; her right hand, on her hip, holds a bunch of leaves(?).

17
Amulet case
Gold with garnets
Ahin Posh, near Jalalabad, Afghanistan; 2nd–3rd century AD
L 12 cm
BM: 1880-29

The openings on this eight-sided cylinder are backed with garnets, as are those on the two ends, one of which can be opened.

Such cylindrical amulet cases, designed to be worn on a cord, can be seen on the chests of the bejewelled Bodhisattvas of the Gandhara period.

PUBLISHED
Tait (ed.), 1986, no. 535.

18
Part of a bracelet
Gold with sapphires
Bodhgaya, Bihar; early centuries AD(?)
DIAM. flowers 2 cm
BM: 1892.3-13 15
Given by Sir Alexander Cunningham

The three gold flowers with sapphire centres are linked by small gold conch shells. This bracelet was part of a deposit in a ball of clay found below the Enlightenment Throne during restoration in 1880–1 at the Mahabodhi Temple, on the site where the Buddha achieved enlightenment.

PUBLISHED·
W. Zwalf (ed.), *Buddhism, Art and Faith,* London, 1985, no. 14.
Tait (ed.), 1986, no. 203.

19 *(overleaf)*
Bulla
Gold
South India, Nilgiri Hills; end of 1st millennium BC(?)
DIAM. 3.2 cm
BM: 1923.7-12.1
Gift of the Elliot family

Made from coins on clay, bullae are often found at ancient Indian sites; the decoration of this one, however, is unique and very much in the Nilgiri style, including the characteristic crescent at the top.

PUBLISHED
Knox, 1985, p. 530, fig. 4 (top middle).
Tait (ed.), 1986, no. 201.

20 *(overleaf)*
Ear-ornament(?)
Gold
South India, Nilgiri Hills; end of 1st millennium BC(?)
DIAM. 2 cm
BM: 1886.5-15.6
Gift of Sir Walter Elliot

These stylised blossoms are made from granules and pellets of gold, with tiny sheets of gold bent into high relief, mounted on a sheet of gold cut into the form of petals.

PUBLISHED
Knox, 1985, p. 529, fig. 4 (middle row).
Tait (ed.), 1986, no. 202.

21 *(overleaf)*
Pendant
Gold
South India, Nilgiri Hills; probably second half of 1st millennium AD
W 1.3 cm
BM: 1886.5-15.2
Gift of Sir Walter Elliot

The back plate of this minute pendant is scalloped out as in no. 24.

PUBLISHED
Knox, 1985, p. 532, fig. 4 (lower right).

22 *(overleaf)*
Bead
Gold
South India, Nilgiri Hills; c. 2nd century BC
DIAM. 1.2 cm (individual beads D 40 mm)
BM: 1886.5-15.5
Gift of Sir Walter Elliot

Beads of this type are composed of small gold balls luted together (the moniliform technique) and then bent into a circle. Closely packed around a relatively thick core, the final result is a solid, roughly-textured tubular bracelet or necklace.

These beads are the only items amongst the Nilgiri Hills material whose date and cultural background are known with any degree of certainty. Identical beads gathered into a bracelet were found at a megalithic grave site near Pondicherry dated to the second century BC. Pondicherry is in Tamilnadu, on the coast south of Madras (J-M. and G. Casal, *Site urbain et sites funéraires des environs de Pondichéry,* Paris, 1956).

PUBLISHED
Knox, 1985, p. 526, fig. 1 (right hand column).

22 · *Jewellery in Indian Sculpture*

21 19 20
23 22
25 24

23
Sunburst ornament (brooch?)
Gold set with a cabochon stone
South India, Nilgiri Hills; date uncertain
DIAM. 2.6 cm
BM: 1886.5-15.10
Gift of Sir Walter Elliot

The stone is surrounded by a complicated and very distinctive arrangement of granules and thin gold strips, all mounted on a flat gold plate.

PUBLISHED
Knox, 1985, pp. 529–30, fig. 4 (top right).

24
Pendant
Sheet gold, partly worked in repoussé
South India, Nilgiri Hills; probably second half of 1st millennium AD
DIAM. 2.5 cm
BM: 1886.5-15.3
Gift of Sir Walter Elliot

An original use of 'the curl and crescent in the local style' (Knox, 1985, p. 532), with the back plate 'scalloped at the edges, in a leaf-like pattern'. (*Ibid*. See also no. 21). These beautifully worked and conceived gold jewels are amongst a group from the same source, of which some pieces have close affinities with finds elsewhere in south India (no. 22), and may well be of local manufacture.

PUBLISHED
Knox, 1985, pp. 524-533.

25
Pipal leaf on chain
Gold
South India, Nilgiri Hills; most likely second half of first millennium AD
L 6.3 cm
BM: 1886.5-15.15
Gift of Sir Walter Elliot

The heart-shaped leaf of the pipal tree *(Ficus religiosa)* occurs very frequently in Indian art, particularly that associated with the Buddhist faith; the Buddha was seated under a pipal tree at Bodhgaya when he achieved illumination. Pipal leaves as ornaments at the end of chains are often shown on stone and metal images of gods and goddesses. For examples from places as far distant from each other as Bihar and Tamilnadu, see Claudine Bautze-Picron, *La sculpture en pierre du Bihar méridional du 8ᵉ au 12ᵉ siècle – la stèle,* unpublished doctoral thesis, Université d'Aix-en-Provence, 1988, no. 75, p. 573; Douglas Barrett, *Early Cola Bronzes,* Bombay, 1965, pl. 22 and pl. 23, reverse. The minute size of this pendant suggests it was made as part of the detachable jewellery of a bronze or wooden image; alternatively it may have been a pendant from a larger piece of jewellery, such as a head ornament (see P. Pal, 1986, p. 55).

26
Medallion-disc with Hariti
Gold repoussé and carnelian
Taxila(?), Panjab; Kushana period, 1st–2nd century AD(?)
D 4.8 cm
IS 9-1948
Formerly collection Col. D. H. Gordon

The goddess wears a short Hellenistic blouse and a diadem as worn by western classical deities. She holds an open lotus blossom in her right hand and a highly stylised cornucopia, one of her attributes, in her left, topped by a vase of fruits identified as pomegranates. There is an almost identical medallion in the Cleveland Museum of Art, the only difference being its slightly larger size and the fact that the lotus blossom is tilted upwards (Czuma, 1985, pp. 75–6.). Two medallion-discs with repoussé busts of Athena and Artemis are in the Art Museum, Princeton University, and are believed to be of the late third or early second century BC; although more elaborate, they are similar in conception (*Greek Gold*, 1965, figs. 92a and b).

PUBLISHED
Ashton, 1947–8, no. 193 (169); Hallade, 1968, p. 97, pl. XI (image reversed).
Doshi, 1985, p. i (image reversed).

Gold Coins

Joe Cribb
Curator of South Asian Coins
British Museum

27
Gold stater of Kushana King Kanishka I
North-west India; early 2nd century AD
BM: CM 1922-4-24-64
Ex R.B. Whitehead Collection

The back of this coin shows a standing image of the Indian deity Shiva, named in Bactrian on the coin as *Oesho*. Shiva is depicted with four arms holding (in clockwise order) a trident, a buck, a waterpot and elephant goad, a hand-drum. The symbol to his left is a Kushana royal symbol.

28
Gold dinar of Gupta King Samudragupta I
North India; mid-4th century AD
BM: CM BMC20
Ex J. Prinsep Collection

The front of this coin shows Samudragupta holding a bow in his left hand and with his right making sacrifice at an altar surmounted by a Garuda standard, symbolising the deity Vishnu. His name *Samudra* is written under his raised arm in a Brahmi script monogram.

29
Gold dinar of Gupta King Samudragupta I
North India; mid-4th century AD
BM: CM BMC57
Ex A. Cunningham Collection

The front of this coin shows a horse tied to a sacrificial post. According to ancient Indian custom only a universal ruler had the right to perform a ritual horse sacrifice *(ashvamedha)*. By issuing a coin with this design Samudragupta was proclaiming himself a universal king. The Brahmi legend is in verse and can be translated as follows: 'The king of kings, of irresistible prowess, having protected the earth, wins heaven'.

30
Gold dinar of Gupta King Chandragupta II
North India; 380-414 AD
BM: CM BMC116
Ex H.N. Wright Collection

The back of this coin shows the Indian goddess Lakshmi seated on the back of a lion, holding a lotus in her left hand and a royal diadem in the other. The design is intended to represent divine support for Chandragupta's kingship. The Brahmi inscription names the king as *siṅhavikramah* (brave as a lion).

31
Gold dinar of Gupta King Kumaragupta I
North India; 414-55 AD
BM: CM BMC250
Ex Nathan Collection

The back of this coin shows the deity Karttikeya seated on his peacock Paravani. This god is shown holding a spear in his left hand and is making a sacrifice at a small altar with the other. The Brahmi inscription names Kumaragupta *Mahendrakumāra*.

Gold Coins · 25

32
Base gold dinar of King Shashanka of Gauda
Bengal; early 7th century AD
BM: CM BMC606
Ex A. Cunningham Collection

The front of this coin shows the god Shiva riding on the back of his bull Nandi. The inscription gives a title of *Śaśāṅka jaya*, victorious. Buddhist tradition records Shashanka's persecution of Buddhism and his destruction of the tree under which the Buddha received enlightenment.

33
Gold coin of Kalachuri King Gangeyadeva of Tripuri
North India; 1015-40 AD
BM: CM 1853.3-1.394
Ex Eden Collection

The front of this coin shows a seated image of the goddess Lakshmi. The goddess is depicted with four arms, holding lotus flowers in her upper arms.

34
Gold coin of the Rashtrakutas of Kanauj
Central India; 11th century AD
BM: CM 1981.6-19.1

The front of this coin shows a standing figure of the Indian deity Rama, holding a bow and an arrow, with a bird and a lotus at his feet. The *devanagari* inscription to his left and right names the god *Srī Rāma*.

35
Gold pagoda of the Eastern Chalukya King Rajaraja
South-east India; c. 1019-60 AD
BM: CM 1879.10-6.1
Ex M. Foster Collection

The front of this coin is stamped with seven punches. The six outer punches make up a Telegu-Kanarese inscription *Śrī Rājarāja Sa 3*, Lord Rajaraja, year 3. The central punch shows a boar, representing the boar incarnation of the Indian deity Vishnu, seal of the Chalukya king of Vengi.

36
Gold mohur of the Mughal Emperor Nur al-Din Jahangir
Minted at Ajmer; dated 1023 AH/1614 AD
BM: CM BMC319
Ex India Office Collection

The front of this coin shows a portrait of Jahangir, seated on a low throne, drinking wine. The Persian legend is written in verse: 'Destiny has drawn on money of gold/The portrait of His Majesty Shah Jahangir'.

Jewellery of the Mughal Period

The Treasury of the World

Foreign travellers coming to India in the fifteenth, sixteenth and seventeenth centuries were dazzled by the splendour of the jewellery worn at the various courts, and intrigued by the array of ornaments worn by people at all levels of society.

The ambassador sent by Shah Rukh from Samarkand, itself no artistic backwater, to Vijayanagar in 1438, notes that 'all the inhabitants of this country, both those of exalted rank and of an inferior class, down to the artisans of the bazaar, wear pearls, or rings adorned with precious stones, in their ears, on their necks, on their arms, on the upper part of the hand and on the fingers.'[1] Ludovica de Varthema, the Italian in India from 1503 to 1508, went to Bijapur, in the Deccan, and said of the Muslim ruler's servants: 'A great number wear on the insteps of their shoes, rubies and diamonds, and other jewels; so you may imagine how many are worn on the fingers of the hand and in the ears.'[2] Passing through the Hindu kingdom of Vijayanagar he exclaimed that the king's horse was 'worth more than some of our cities, on account of the ornaments which it wears.'[3] The king of Calicut's jewels were 'a wonder to behold'; Duarte Barbosa, the Portuguese official in Calicut a few years later, describes the multiplicity of gold ornaments worn by the thousand 'ladies of good caste' in the king's service.[4] In addition, descriptions abound of gilt pillars in buildings, jewelled golden thrones, and roofs and walls of plated gold, all of which explains why India could be described by François Bernier as 'an abyss of gold.'

Sadly, very little gold jewellery has survived to show the exact nature of the ornaments which led Sir Thomas Roe to describe the Mughal Court as 'the treasury of the world'. Visual evidence for Mughal jewellery depends at first entirely on the paintings executed for the third emperor, Akbar (r. 1556–1605), mostly dating from the last two decades of his reign. The style of jewellery worn from the foundation of the empire in 1526 until the late sixteenth century can so far only be guessed at.[5]

Strangely, there is a complete imbalance between the travellers' descriptions, corroborated by contemporary Mughal accounts of the wealth of the empire and the striking lack of jewellery worn in, for example, the scenes of Akbar at court (fig. 5). In these, the emperor wears simple necklaces, occasionally a thumb or finger ring, and turban jewels which are either plain gold, or gold and gem-encrusted bands, or holders for plumes of feathers. The court dignitaries are virtually unadorned. The contrast between this apparent austerity and William Hawkins' early seventeenth-century description of the Mughal treasury is startling. In a section entitled 'The ornaments of gold', he begins: 'of brooches for their heads, wherinto their feathers be put, these be very rich, and of them there are two thousand ... ringes with jewels of rich diamonds, ballace rubies [i.e. spinels],

Fig. 5
The emperor Akbar watching dancing girls.
Opaque watercolour on paper
From an illustrated manuscript of the *Akbarnama*; Mughal, c. 1590
V&A: IS 2–1896 16/117

rubies, and old emerods [emeralds] there is an infinite number, which only the keeper thereof knoweth.'[6]

The treasury for unmounted stones was so vast that a treasurer and two assistants were employed full time solely to administer it; no diamonds were kept that were under two-and-a-half carats in weight. Hawkins relates a story told to him by a diamond-cutter friend: the friend had asked for a 'foule', or flawed diamond, to make into a powder with which to cut another large diamond: 'They brought him a chest ... of three spannes long and a spanne and a half broad, and a spanne and a half deepe, full of diamants of all sizes and sorts; yet he could find never any one for his purpose, but one of five rotties, which was not very foule neither.'[7]

In order that the emperor might see this vast store of jewels, everything was divided into 360 parts, so that he could examine a certain number every day.

Akbar's own style of jewellery was a hybrid of Iranian and Hindu influences, as would be expected of the emperor of a dynasty whose cultural roots were in Iran, but which had ruled northern India since 1526. The turban plume (*kalgī* or *jīgha*) and golden bands (*sarpīch*) are exactly those seen in contemporary Safavid painting; his necklaces on the other hand are of the kinds listed in Kautilya's *Arthashastra*, consisting of pearls, pearls and gems, gold on its own, or gold with pearls and gems.[8]

A contemporary work, the *A'in-i Akbari*, part of a compendious account of the empire including everything from its history to the rules governing the fodder

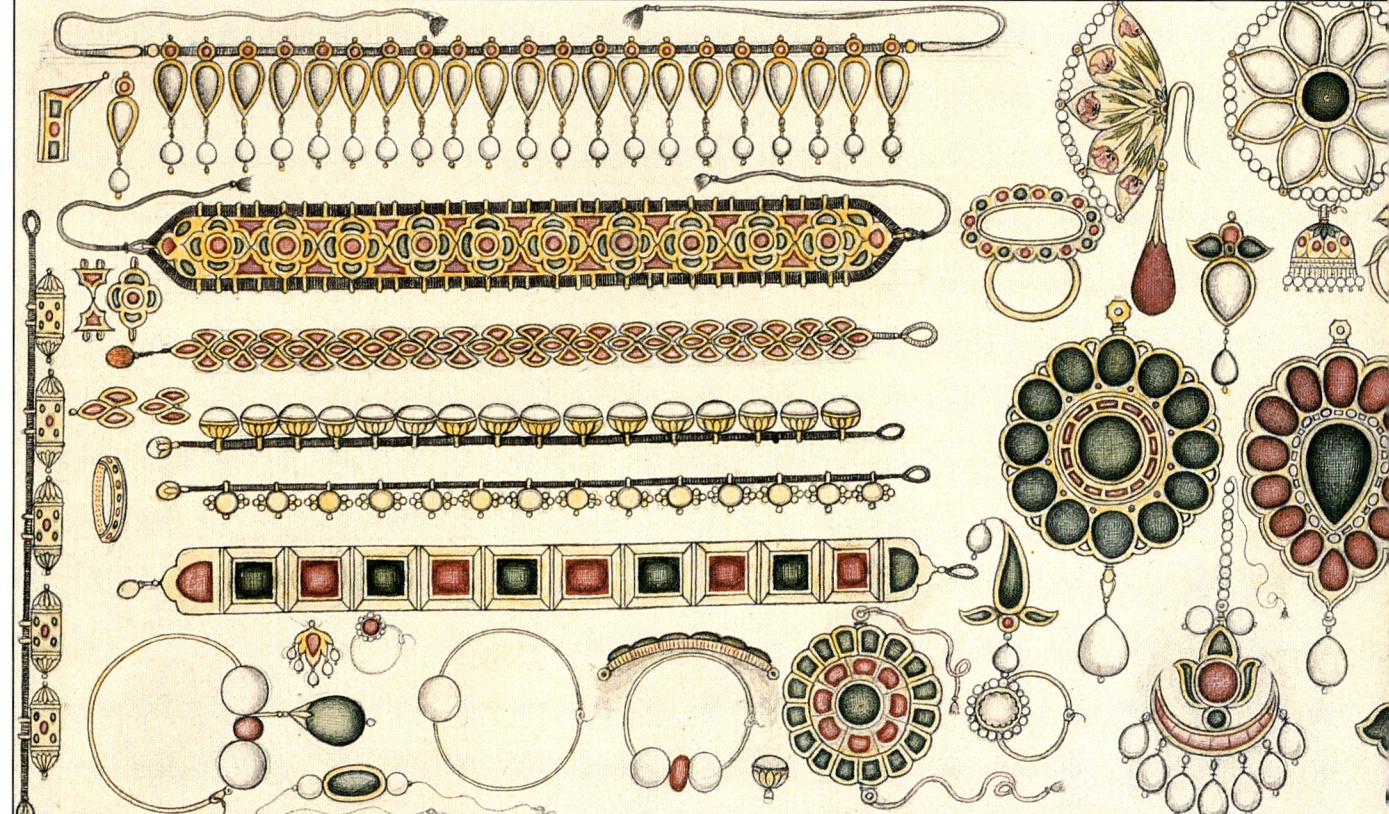

Fig. 6
Illustration of jewellery from an album compiled for Colonel J.B. Gentil at Faizabad in 1774. Watercolour
V&A: IS 25–1980 f.48

allowed in the imperial stables, gives a list of ornaments worn by the women of Hindustan.[9] Some of these may be seen, virtually unchanged and by this time worn equally by Muslim ladies, in the Gentil album of 1774 (fig. 6), such as the *karanphūl* ('earflower') which is shaped like the blossom of love-in-the-mist (*Nigella sativa*, or *Nigella indica*), and *nāth* (nose ring). The *nāth* (in the form of a circular gold wire threaded with a ruby between two pearls, or other gemstones), though clearly commonplace by the time Abu'l Fazl compiled his list, seems to be a foreign interloper. It does not appear in the sculpture or painting of the pre-Islamic period and there is no word for it in Sanskrit literature. Most scholars presume, therefore, that it arrived with the Muslim incursions of the twelfth century onwards.[10]

P. K. Gode records the earliest representation of nose rings known so far, in the mural paintings of the Tiruvambadi shrine in the Shri Padmanabhasvami temple, Trivandrum, South India, which has an inscription giving the date of construction as 1374-5[11]. The earliest European reference to nose rings also notes their use in the south, in Vijayanagar. Duarte Barbosa says of the women: 'In the side of one of the nostrils they make a small hole, through which they put a fine wire with a pearl, sapphire or ruby pendant.'[12]

Other types, such as the *mang* 'worn on the parting of the hair to add to its beauty' and *bālī*, 'a circlet with a pearl worn through the ear' were worn throughout the period. The few images of ladies at Akbar's court show that the divisions marking Indian and Iranian jewellery may have been observed more clearly than

in the case of the emperor's ornaments; the dancers in the illustration from the *Akbarnama* of c. 1590 (fig. 6) are both Muslim and Hindu and wear clearly differentiated styles of jewellery in accordance with their origins.

The same section of the *A'in-i Akbari* contains a description of the technical skills of the Hindu goldsmiths.[13] Each skill was practised by a specialist craftsman, which meant that an engraved, enamelled and gem-set gold object would be passed from one to another in the royal *karkhana*, or workshop, before being complete. Each craftsman was paid on a scale related to the weight of the object which, in the case of the larger pieces, was often scratched on to the bottom.

The inlayer, or *zar nishan*, was given pride of place in the list: he engraved materials of many kinds including hardstone, steel and ivory. The enameller, or *minakar*, worked 'on cups, flagons, rings and other articles with gold and silver'; this appears to be the earliest known reference to enamelling in India. Other craftsmen did 'plain', pierced or repoussé work, plaited wire, made gold leaf and applied niello. The *charmkar* is of particular interest: he 'incrusts granulations of gold and silver like poppy seeds on ornaments and vessels'. It is clear from this that the subcontinent must have had a continuous history of granulation from early times until the nineteenth century (see nos. 3 and 58), unlike the west where the technique brought to perfection by the Etruscans was lost until its revival in the mid-nineteenth century.

The technique which is quintessentially Indian is the setting of stones by means of *kundan*, the other technique listed by Abu'l Fazl. Mughal jewellery is rarely solid gold, having a core of lac, a natural resin. The pieces which will make up the finished object are first shaped by the relevant craftsman (and soldered together if the shape is complicated) and left in separate, hollow halves. Holes are cut for the stones, any engraving or chasing is carried out, and the pieces are enamelled. When the stones are to be set, lac is inserted in the back, and is then visible from the front through the holes for the stones. Highly refined gold, the *kundan*, is then used to cover that lac and the stone is pushed into the *kundan*. More *kundan* is applied round the edges to strengthen the setting and to give it a neater appearance. This was the only method of setting gems into gold in the Mughal period until claw settings were introduced in the nineteenth century via Western jewellery.

Given all this information, the lack of jewellery in the miniatures of the period is inexplicable; the techniques were available for a sophisticated array of ornaments, and the treasury virtually overflowed with suitable raw materials. Moreover, one of Akbar's wives was keenly interested in the artistic creations of the workshops: Abu'l Fazl concludes: 'Her Majesty has suggested new patterns in each kind.'[14]

By the time Akbar's son, Jahangir, came to the throne, fashions at court had undergone a dramatic transformation as can be seen in the painting of Jahangir weighing his son, Prince Khurram (fig. 8). The lavishness of the emperor's appearance in miniature paintings now accords well with contemporary descriptions, such as those given by Sir Thomas Roe, the ambassador sent to the court by James I of England.[15] The wealth of the empire is now overwhelmingly obvious and Jahangir's voracious appetite for 'raretyes' from abroad can be seen to influence jewellery forms and motifs. The Agra factors of the East India Company,

Fig. 7
Dancing girls and musicians performing at a marriage entertainment.
Opaque watercolour on paper
From an illustrated manuscript of the *Akbarnama*; Mughal, c.1590
V&A: IS 2–1896 16/117

32 · Jewellery of the Mughal Period

informing the Court of Directors in London of commodities which would find a guaranteed market in Mughal India, note: 'We never heard of any commodity the Portingalls [Portuguese] doe bringe to Goa than Jewells, ready money and some few other provisions ... Those factors which came from Goa to the Court, Agra and Brampore, bringe nothinge but Jewells.'[16] Jahangir's close friend Mukarrab Khan, Governor of Surat, collecting items to please the emperor from the ports of Cambay and Surat, presented 'jewels and jewelled things, and vessels of gold and silver made in Europe.'[17] The presents were so extensive that they were laid before Jahangir for two and a half months, the emperor condescendingly noting that 'most of them were pleasing to me'.

Foreign artefacts were clearly reaching the court in large numbers and being copied by the artisans in the same way as the painters copied paintings brought by the Jesuits and Sir Thomas Roe. European craftsmen were also employed at the court; Jahangir's memoirs make reference to one he called Hunarmand 'who had no rival in the arts of a goldsmith and a jeweller, and in all sorts of skill' and who had made a gold and silver throne 'much ornamented and decorated'.[18]

One of the earliest pieces of Mughal jewellery to survive shows creeping Europeanisation; the scrolling leaf designs on the inner surface of a thumb ring of a type seen in the V&A *Akbarnama* of c. 1590, and dating to twenty or so years later, are influenced by Renaissance jewellery (no. 93). A more significant European intrusion can be seen in turban jewellery where a completely new form seems to have its source in European hat aigrettes.

Turban jewellery was the prerogative of the emperor, his close family, or members of his entourage (including his horse). Akbar, as we have seen, followed Iranian fashion by having his upright feather plume at the front of the turban. Jahangir introduced his own, softer, style with the plume weighted down with a large pearl (see fig. 8). His son, Shah Jahan, seems to have turned to Europe for an innovative *jīgha* which relates to the designs of the Dutch jeweller Arnold Lulls (fig. 9). Lulls supplied jewels to the English court between 1603 and 1606; Shah Jahan would have seen similar jewels worn by James I in the portraits brought to the court by Sir Thomas Roe. In the 1618 painting Shah

Fig. 8 (opposite)
Jahangir weighing Prince Khurram on his sixteenth birthday.
Opaque watercolour on paper
Mughal; c. 1615–25
BM: 1948.10–9.069

Fig. 9
Page from an album of jewellery drawings showing two jewelled aigrettes.
Pencil, pen and ink, wash, body colour and gold on paper
Workshop of Arnold Lulls; c. 1610
V&A: D 6–1896

Fig. 10 (opposite)
Shah Jahan as a prince
Opaque watercolour on paper
Mughal; c.1616–17
V&A: IM 14-1925

Jahan, still a prince, holds an Indianised version of Lulls' designs (fig. 10), but it is not until 1628 when Shah Jahan came to the throne, that this style is seen in miniatures. It seems, therefore, to be Shah Jahan's own emblem.

By the time of his successor Aurangzeb, however, the form was ubiquitous and, as in the reign of Shah Jahan, was used to display the finest gems of the Mughal treasury. François Bernier describes Aurangzeb's aigrette as being 'composed of diamonds of an extraordinary size and value, beside an oriental topaz, which may be pronounced unparalleled, exhibiting a lustre like the sun.'[19]

The use of turban jewels interestingly mirrors the decline of Mughal authority and the rise in importance of the provincial courts. Although Aurangzeb succeeded where his father, grandfather and great-grandfather had failed, and defeated the sultans of the Deccan, the campaigns drained the resources of the empire and overstretched its administrative capability. Aurangzeb's grip seems to have loosened on every level; turban jewels were now presented to nobles as well as to members of the royal family, but even then the recipients became over-presumptuous. In 1693 he was forced to issue an order that 'no amir to whom a *sarpech* of jewellery was granted should wear it except on Sunday; they should not wrap their head [with any unauthorised *sarpech*].'[20] Under his feeble successor Shah ʿAlam Bahadur Shah, the situation worsened; a contemporary historian complained: 'Since the rise of the House of Timur it had been the rule that one and the same title should not be given to two persons; but now the ugly practice arose of giving the same title to two or more persons, and … grants of … the *jīgha* and *sarpech* were no longer regulated by the rank and dignity of the recipient.'[21]

Provincial rulers took over stock imperial imagery in the way they were depicted in painting, for example in the Murshidabad miniature of the ruling Nawab ʿAliverdi Khan. He holds out a turban jewel to his grandson and designated successor, Siraj ad-Daula, in conscious imitation of the Mughals (fig. 11).

Fig. 11
The Nawab ʿAliverdi Khan of Bengal and companions
Opaque watercolour on paper
Murshidabad; c.1750–75
V&A: D.1201-1903

36 · *Jewellery of the Mughal Period*

Fig. 12
Maharana Bhim Singh with a hawk
Opaque water colour and gold on cloth
Udaipur, Rajasthan; c.1815-20
Ashmolean Museum; 1985.31

The jewel is almost identical to that given to Admiral Watson in 1757 by Mir Ja'far, the Nawab who ousted Siraj ad-Daula with British help (see no. 37). Other eighteenth-century types can be seen in the group which came from the Jaipur treasury (nos. 38-41; no. 43); at least one of these (no. 38) may be a purely Rajput form, judging by its general similarity to that worn by Bhim Singh (fig. 12).

In 1739, Delhi was sacked by the Iranian ruler Nadir Shah, and the *de facto* devolution of the empire was accelerated. Much of what was taken, including mounds of uncut gemstones, some engraved with the names of the Mughal emperors, became part of the crown jewels of Iran.[22] Other pieces, jewels and gold vessels encrusted with rubies, diamonds and emeralds, or enamelled, were presented to Russia by Nadir Shah in 1741 and are now in the Hermitage.[23]

The provincial rulers were then able to hold sway with little interference from the centre, although at least nominal allegiance to Delhi was maintained. Courtly jewellery carried on the traditions established in the seventeenth century, as may be seen by comparing jewellery shown in paintings of the period with the Gentil album of 1774. Certain regional variations, nevertheless, developed. Particular schools of enamelling, for instance, may be identified, though as yet considerably fewer than the number which must have existed.

The court of Oudh, at Faizabad until 1775 when it moved to Lucknow, had by the mid-seventeenth century established its own style of vibrant translucent blue and green enamelling on silver. Though the use of silver is somewhat unusual, the champlevé technique is that used in all Indian enamelling except for the Iranian-derived painted examples. A magnificent *huqqa*, once belonging to Robert Clive and in a 1766 inventory[24], is probably Oudh work. In the nineteenth century, pieces made for exhibitions from 1851 onwards and now in the Victoria and Albert Museum, show that blue and green were still the keynote colours, but that a soft, pale, translucent violet and a slightly harsh, opaque gamboge yellow had been added, together with both opaque and translucent turquoise.

According to Rai Krishnadasa[25] the polychrome painted enamel of Iran was introduced to Oudh during the reign of Asaf ad-Daula (1775-97) by Kaisar Agha, an enameller arriving from Kabul. The dusky rose-pink of the palette seems to have particularly appealed to the Indian enamellers and became dominant (see no. 96). The style became a speciality of the Benares enamellers, who took it with them to Delhi. It disappeared from Benares in 1923 when the last hereditary master, Babbu Singh, died.

Iranian enamelling was also found at Hyderabad under the Talpur rulers of Sindh: here the influence was direct, Iranian masters merely carrying out their work under a different patron. The colours are much more vivid than those of Benares, with yellows and oranges vibrating against pink. Even there, however, a softer, more 'pink' style seems to have evolved, judging by the signed and dated enamelled dagger and scabbard which appeared on the art market in 1987.[26]

Jaipur was the enamelling centre *par excellence* in the eighteenth and nineteenth centuries, the craftsmen traditionally being thought to have come from Lahore. Here the colour scheme is firmly within the Mughal tradition. The red and green flowers on a plain white ground derive from the white marble architecture of the first half of the seventeenth century, inlaid with flowers of jade and carnelian.

These are copied on some of the finest goldsmiths' work to have been produced under Mughal patronage.[27] These colours were by no means exclusive to Jaipur, being found on much eighteenth-century jewellery from centres as far apart as Murshidabad (no. 37) and the Deccan.[28]

The enamel work of Lahore is so far only known from the rather inferior work on the backs of the 'orders of merit' introduced by Ranjit Singh, made in emulation of the French Légion d'Honneur worn by one of his military advisers (no. 64).

During the eighteenth century, the artistic productions of most of the empire had their foundation entirely in Mughal aesthetics. Some areas, such as Rajasthan, were able to resist being completely overwhelmed, thought it is difficult to isolate specifically Rajput forms or motifs on unprovenanced jewellery. This is because Rajasthan undoubtedly contributed a great deal to the formation of the hybrid Mughal style: its princesses married Mughal royalty and its rulers had taken high positions at court, both bringing their jewellery and, probably, their craftsmen with them. The Rajputs had also contributed, willingly or not, jewelled and gold articles to the emperor's treasury.

In Rajasthan itself, the local character is, as would be expected, more apparent: there are, for example, restrictions on the use of certain types of gold jewellery. In general, (as in the south) gold is not worn on the feet by Hindus as it is a sacred metal which would thus be defiled. Hendley, however, notes that in Rajasthan 'the anklet of gold [worn by men] worn on one or both feet is a proof of nobility as well as of being entitled to a certain position at a Durbar, and to certain honours when there.'[29] He quotes the passage in Tod's *Annals and Antiquities of Rajasthan* where, after the siege of Chitor, the equivalent of 170lb of gold bangles or anklets were found on the bodies of the men who had fallen, 'all the men who wore them having been of noble-blood or knights'.

The South

However little the jewellery of Mughal India has been studied, the neglect of southern India has been far greater. Ironically, the scope for such a study is enormous: unlike the north, where similar forms are found across a wide area and changed relatively slowly across the decades, south Indian sculptures (and, to a lesser extent, paintings) reveal marked shifts in jewellery fashions, many with strongly regional characteristics. If analysis of these could be undertaken, comparison with temple collections of jewellery should eventually enable a far more detailed history of south Indian jewellery to be produced than could be the case with Mughal ornaments.

At its simplest level, south Indian jewellery imitates forms found in nature, as Havell demonstrated in his articles on jewellery from the Madras Presidency.[30] Chased gold is made to imitate the *rudraksha* bead sacred to the god Shiva (no.91), elements of necklaces may copy cut grass stalks, lotus buds, garlic bulbs or lentils as well as flowers. Nevertheless, the jewellery of the area is also characterised by its extreme complexity of structure, or combination of motifs. A flat sheet of gold may be decorated with an almost bewildering assortment of minute soldered

Fig. 13 (opposite above)
From left to right: A Bania couple; a Chetti couple; a Kanarese couple.
Opaque watercolour on paper
Tanjore, South India; from a Company album of c.1830.
V&A: IS 39-1987 f.4

Fig. 14 (opposite below)
From left to right: A Muslim *zamindar* and his wife; a Rajput couple; a Muslim betel-nut seller and his wife.
Opaque watercolour on paper
Tanjore, South India; from a Company album of c.1830.
V&A: IS 39-1987 f.5

The South · 39

40 · *Jewellery of the Mughal Period*

pieces of twisted or plaited wire, tiny flattened discs and granules arranged in groups and built out by adding more on top, as seen on the ear pendant (no. 57). The *naga* ear ornaments (no. 58) are a mixture of formally arranged geometric elements, the squares grouped together at the front of the circular base, and a naturalistic cobra-hood which develops, bizarrely, into a bat-like creature with fangs. The intricacy of these motifs would be lost to the outsider: the miniature scale would not allow them to be carefully observed and the ear ornaments are worn as a group, clustered together with four others.[31] This kind of jewellery is not easily accessible to those outside the culture that produces it. The characteristic arrangements of stones in grid patterns are an abstraction of timeless features found in temple architecture. Thus, the twelve rubies which surround the pearl Nandi (no. 100) suggests the *rasi mandala,* or Zodiac ceiling panels of the kind found, for instance, in the twelfth century Subrahmanya temple at Pollachi in Coimbatore.[32] The nine stones at the centre of the forehead ornament probably from Madras (no. 48) are the *navaratna* (see no. 82) but the arrangement is again that to be found in temple architecture (for instance in the seventeenth-century Adikesava temple in Thiruvattaru, Kanyakumari district).[33] Again, the parrots pecking lotuses seen in the sixteenth-century Bhuvaraha temple in Shrimushnam are a motif still found in nineteenth-century jewellery (no. 92).[34] Technically, jewellery of the south differs greatly from that of the Mughal-influenced areas of India. The precious metal acts both as support and decoration; enamel is not usually found and gemstones tend to be used for their symbolic value rather than primarily for their decorative effect. Sheet gold is far more in evidence than in Mughal jewellery: a thick flat band may be used for an armlet, with flat lozenges set at an angle to support three-dimensional parrots and a jewelled flower (no. 92). The ring from the Castellani collection (no. 103) has first been shaped from sheet gold: the jewelled sections are then applied on top but do not alter the outline established by the support. The gold Nandi ring (no. 99) is formed rather differently as its gold-covered hoop has a core probably made from lac, but relies entirely on manipulation of the surface of the gold, or on applied gold, for its decoration. The sapphire Nandi ring (no. 101) illustrates the symbolic use of gemstones: the bull is the mount of Shiva and the stone suggests the colour of the god's skin, as he is commonly depicted in painting. Sapphire is a stone often thought by Hindus to bring misfortune. Tagore describes how some jewellers would keep a stone 'on trial' for several days before they would commit themselves to purchasing it.[35] Two imperfections on the sapphire bull have been gouged out with no attempt to disguise the marks; once these flaws were removed the stone's malevolent influence was presumably nullified.

South Indian jewellery often shows considerable monumentality, as can be seen in the so-called 'Hawking Ring of Tipu Sultan.' The ring was in the collection of Henry Cornwallis Neville, the fourth Baron Braybrooke. The architect and designer, William Burges, sketched it, possibly in 1870, the date on the drawing of an armlet which appears next to it in Burges' album (fig. 15).

The caption associates it with Tipu Sultan, the Muslim ruler of Mysore from 1782 until he was defeated by the British at the siege of Seringapatam in 1799. The ring was, according to a catalogue of the Braybrooke collection held in the

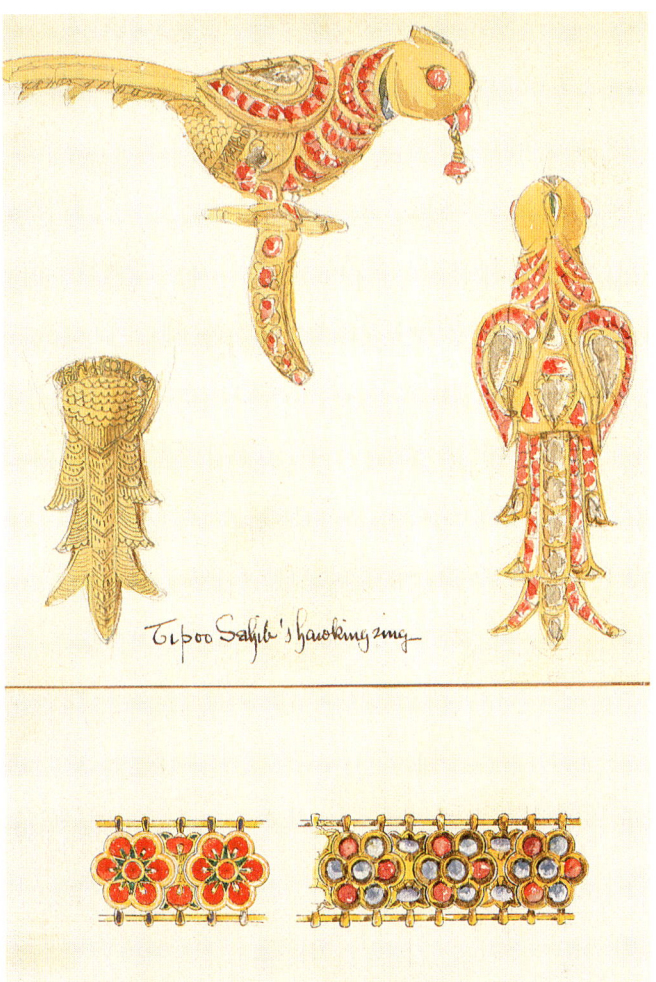

Fig. 15
Drawings of Indian jewellery
Watercolour and pencil
William Burges; c.1870
Royal Institute of British
Architects: from Burges' album of
Metalwork drawings, f.59 (recto).

Department of Mediaeval and Later Antiquities at the British Museum, taken at the first siege, in 1792.[36] Though the ring was, in all probability, owned by Tipu Sultan, it is unlikely to have been made for him. Burges' drawing shows a *devanagari* inscription on the breast of the bird; this is confirmed by the British Museum catalogue which shows it more clearly, though not clearly enough for it to be deciphered. The catalogue entry notes that the inscription includes the word 'Maharaja'. The combination of the Hindu title and the *devanagari* script rule this out as a product of the Mysore *karkhana*: the court used the cultural language of the day, Persian. The many objects which survive in British collections today which definitely were made in Mysore, and in some cases specifically for Tipu Sultan [37] are inscribed exclusively in Persian, with Arabic if the inscription has a religious content. The ring must, therefore, have been taken from a nearby Hindu ruler on one of the many campaigns undertaken by him, or by his father Haider ᶜAli. Nevertheless, the provenance of the ring would make it a key piece in the history of south Indian jewellery; sadly, it was stolen from Audley End, near Saffron Walden, in 1951.

Marriage jewellery occupies an important place in the repertoire of ornaments in the south. The two sisters (fig. 16) and the resentful little girl from Madras in the photographs of 1892 (fig. 17) probably wear their family's best jewellery. Her necklace, or *thālī,* with its pendants composed of auspicious emblems, relates closely to one collected by Caspar Purdon Clarke in 1881 or 1882 (no. 70).

Another impressive marriage necklace (no. 69) illustrates the way in which South Indian jewellery, whilst retaining its own unmistakeable character, could not entirely escape the effects of fashion elsewhere. The repoussé details on the pendants, worked in very high relief, are the source of the *swami* work (no. 122) so popular with the European market in the late nineteenth century. This is superimposed on to a support of abstract shape, whose origins can only be guessed at. Yet above and below the deities are applied panels pierced with scrolling designs that are utterly foreign to southern India and must have come via European jewellery.

Even royal jewellery was subject to alien cultural and formal influences. A series of eighteenth-century wall paintings in a temple in Thanjavur, Tamilnadu,

Fig. 16 (left)
Two girls from Madras.
From a photograph taken in Madras in 1891
Photographer unknown
V&A: Indian Department

Fig. 17 (right)
Detail from a photograph captioned '"chetty girls" Madras, November, 1891'.
Photographer unknown
V&A: Indian Department

depicts both historical episodes in the history of the local rulers, and scenes from the life of the king.[38] The paintings show an interesting array of contemporary Thanjavur jewellery and artefacts, but there is also a surprising Mughal influence. In a few scenes, including a coronation scene, the king is dressed in Mughal attire and turban, replete with turban jewels. The kingdom was also subject to European influence. One of the panels shows Europeans seated in armchairs before the king;[39] another shows two European soldiers offering presents to him. By the time the Ramnad kingdom came under the administration of the British about seventy years later, European influence was beginning to show itself in the jewellery of southern India.

India and the West

In the eighteenth century, the British in India at first consciously adopted the habits and customs of their surroundings, smoking *huqqas* and sometimes wearing the comfortable loose clothing dictated by the climate. In the higher levels of society, it was deemed politically astute to appear in public on equal terms with the nawabs with whom they had contact.

Robert Clive presented gifts of imperial splendour, such as a gold attar box worth 3240 rupees, to the head of the most influential banking concern of the day, Jagath Seth. In 1784, Warren Hastings sent a *khil'at* to the same figure, an act which showed how far the East India Company had moved from being a mere trading organisation. The *khil'at* was a presentation made by the emperor, by a provincial ruler or high ranking dignitary, and consisted of a robe of honour, set of jewellery and other prescribed items, depending on the status of the recipient. Sir John Shore, for similar reasons of ostentation, wore an emerald seal ring (no. 108) to mark his documents rather than following contemporary English usage and having a fob seal. The British themselves were often given a *khil'at*, and these are sometimes depicted in paintings, perhaps worn by their children, for instance in a painting of Admiral Watson and his son (see no. 37); George Clive's child may also be wearing the jewels and costume of a *khil'at* (fig. 18).

Precious stones were collected by Company officials as a means of transporting gains, often ill-gotten, to bank accounts in faraway England, but these were sometimes set into jewellery by local craftsmen. Lady Clive, according to her husband's accounts, had a ruby ring 'country set.' As more European ladies came to India in search of husbands, the demand for locally-made jewellery increased. The desire to follow up-to-date European fashion was strong but was thwarted by the length of time it took to send orders to London by sea and have the required items returned. The solution was to have them made by a European jeweller, such as the one who advertised in William Hicky's Bengal Gazette of 1781: 'John Adie, Lately Arrived from Europe' had set up shop as 'a Working Jeweller' and was 'thoroughly acquainted with setting all kinds of Diamonds, Pearls, etc.' Many other similar concerns are listed in Wynyard Wilkinson's *Register of European Goldsmiths in India*.[40] It was, however, much more likely that the jeweller would be Indian. Not only had the singular ability of the Indian artisans to copy anything been noted by almost every foreign traveller to the subcontinent over the centuries, but it was statistically almost inevitable. Wilkinson gives the intriguing information that in Bombay in 1864 there were 10,670 'Hindoo or other caste' goldsmiths (as well as others of different religions and races) compared with twenty European goldsmiths, while the European population at the time numbered about 9000.[41] This explains why the pieces made, for instance, in Madras in about 1850, though entirely European in form, exhibit small peculiarities when compared with those of western provenance (nos. 114-18). By this time there were much larger businesses run by Europeans, such as Hamilton & Co. of Calcutta and P. Orr & Sons of Madras, which traded in western-style jewellery but employed local craftsmen.

Not all the British ladies wished their jewellery to be European, however. The famous itinerant pilgrim in search of the picturesque, Mrs Fanny Parks, delighted in having ornaments made on the verandah of her bungalow by a visiting goldsmith, or in the local bazaar by her own craftsman, and relished the contrast in taste between herself and her Indian friends. Having had an amulet made for herself in solid silver to repel 'not one, but seventy misfortunes', she wrote: 'No lady in India can wear anything so valueless as silver, of which the ornaments made for her servants are composed.'[42] It was inevitable that, if Indian goldsmiths copied western models, European influence would become apparent in their work for indigenous consumption. Claw settings became commonplace, techniques such as *cannetille* (no. 118) are frequently found, and entirely western forms composed of entirely Indian motifs (nos. 122 and 119) are produced in many centres for tourists or, by the 1850s, 60s and 70s for export to the major international exhibitions.

The exhibitions were the key factor in leading to a reciprocal Indian influence on, particularly, English jewellery. In 1851, London's Great Exhibition exposed the eye of the world to Indian jewellery. The Koh-i-Noor was a major attraction, though its Indian cut disappointed the crowds. In the pale northern light, half concealed within Messrs Chubb's patent diamond case, it had little brilliance and in July 1852, it was, tragically, recut according to western taste. The Indian artefacts on show, however, caused a great stir, epitomising to commentators like Owen Jones 'all the principles, all the unity, all the truth' lacking in the machine-made products of contemporary Europe. Indian jewellery from the exhibition was taken into the collections of the new South Kensington Museum (nos. 84 and 85) and the existing collections of the East India Company's Indian Museum were carefully examined for inspiration. Robert Phillips of Cockspur Street copied the enamelling on an Indian Museum thumb ring to produce a superb necklace for the Paris Exhibition of 1867 (no. 110) and the London jewellers Watherston and Brogden made brooches from imported, unmounted Partabgarh plaquettes.[43] Slightly later, Carlo Giuliano of London produced his own versions of Indian necklaces.[44]

At first, the appreciation of Indian jewellery seems to have been confined largely to the aesthetic circles who patronised Arthur Lazenby Liberty's Regent Street Oriental Warehouse, established in 1875. General pleas were made for a move away from the diamond-laden, mechanically-produced styles popular with the prosperous middle classes, towards jewellery which made less of a statement of wealth and which was entirely hand-crafted. John Ruskin had campaigned for the adoption of the cabochon cut, which was almost always used in Indian

Fig. 18
Detail from a painting of George Clive with his family and an Indian maidservant
Oil on canvas
Joshua Reynolds; c. 1765
Gemäldegalerie, Staatliche Museen Preussischer Kulturbesitz, Berlin (West): 1.1978

46 · *Jewellery of the Mughal Period*

jewellery.[45] Mrs Haweis drew 'the attention of the wealthy public [to] Her Majesty's wise example of sometimes wearing uncut jewels.'[46] Sir Charles Eastlake, in his *Hints on Household Taste,* commended his readers to the 'specimens of really artistic jewellery' to be found in the Indian collections of the South Kensington Museum[47] though his praise of the cabochon cut seems to be based solely on the fact that these irregularly-set stones demonstrate that the piece had been made by hand rather than by the despised machine. Leading figures of the Arts and Crafts movement collected Indian jewellery: Charlotte Gere notes that most of the jewellery listed in a catalogue of effects sold by Dante Gabriel Rossetti is Indian (cf. no. 91) and Holman Hunt also owned Indian pieces.[48]

In 1876 Queen Victoria became Empress of India, and 'Indian jewellery became fashionable in circles beyond the bohemian and artistic world of the Aesthetics.'[49] The *swami* work of P. Orr & Sons of Madras (no. 122), for example, was popular in Britain and many of the items acquired by Caspar Purdon Clarke on his 1881-2 purchasing tour of India on behalf of the South Kensington Museum must have been typical export wares.

The next wave of interest in India came towards the end of the first decade of the twentieth century. In 1910, Diaghilev's production of *Schéhérazade*, and the fashion designer Paul Poiret's party on the theme of the Thousand and One Nights in 1911, contributed to the appearance of a fairy tale 'oriental style' drawing its inspiration at random from India, Iran and the Islamic Near East.[50]

The firm of Cartier provided harmonising jewellery and in 1912 designed an aigrette copying Indian turban jewels. Hans Nadelhofer, the chronicler of the firm, notes that 'Cartier's *sarpech* aigrettes were not only admired at Oriental balls

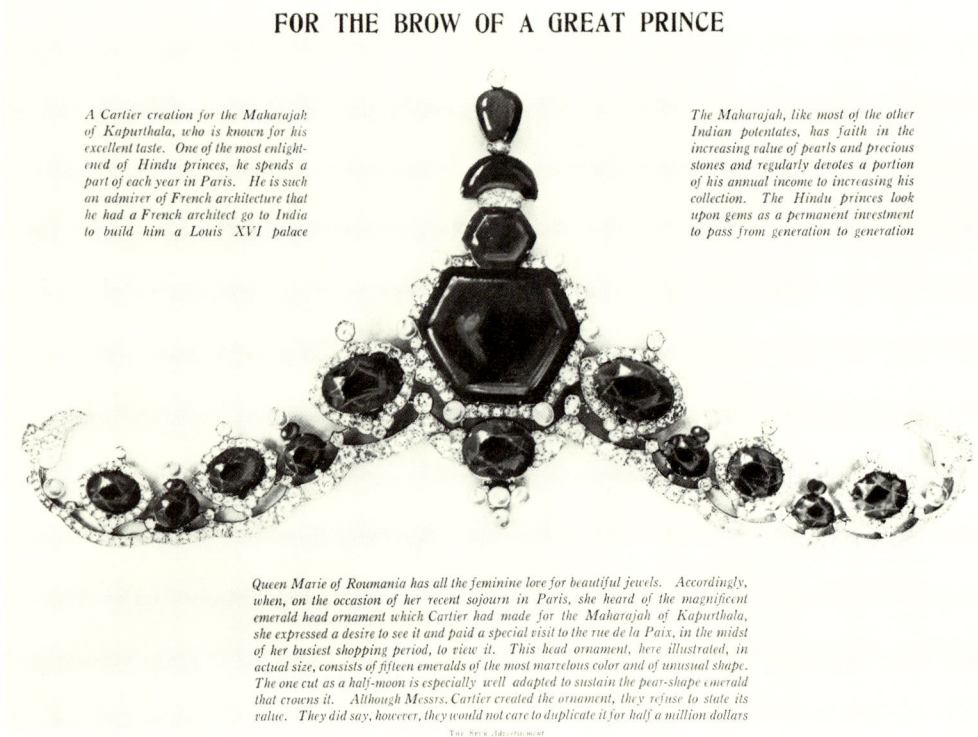

Fig. 19
Advertisement from *The Spur* showing a turban ornament made by Cartier for the Maharajah of Kapurthala in 1926.

in Paris and London but were even bought by the Indian potentates with whom Jacques Cartier did business in London.'[51]

Indian influence was perhaps more keenly felt in the colours used in Cartier's jewellery at this period than in general forms, however. Nadelhofer shows how Fauve influence had led to revolutionary contrasting combinations of sapphires and emeralds, for instance, 'with rock crystal being used as the neutral background in a new contrapuntal handling of colour'; the blue-green match was a particularly daring innovation and was called by Louis Cartier his 'peacock pattern'.[52] Nadelhofer suggests that the source of this combination was the enamelled jewellery of the seventeenth and eighteenth centuries but perhaps the name should simply be taken at face value. Peacock feathers and motifs were very much in favour among Aesthetes, whereas the Indian enamels of the seventeenth and eighteenth centuries characteristically used red, white and green, with small touches of blue or other colours, and Lucknow blue and green would not have been widely known.

At this period, the firm of Cartier had a specific impact on Indian jewellery. From 1909, all aspects of the firm's Indian business, such as buying stones, were conducted through the London house, by Jacques Cartier. In 1911 he went to Delhi for George V's Coronation durbar, and there made his first important contacts with the Maharajas.[53] His eye for things Indian was trained by Imre Schwaiger, the leading Delhi dealer, who looked after the firm's interests in Delhi and sold them Indian jewellery (the V&A also bought some of its best objects from him at the same time). As European high society became obsessed with orientalism, its Indian equivalent turned to the West (fig. 19). Cartier was asked to model collections of jewellery in fashionable Paris styles and caused a fundamental revolution in taste: gold was, probably for the first time in Indian history, spurned. The Gaekwar of Baroda, Sayaji Rao III 'commissioned Jacques Cartier to reset his entire collection in platinum, then more prized than either gold or Indian enamel work in the westernised courts of India.'[54] It is significant that it was at this period that the Maharaja of Jaipur sold some of his jewellery which, being with one exception entirely enamelled, could not be refashioned (nos. 38 ff.). The crown jewels of Patiala were also remodelled, and Nadelhofer aptly remarks that 'it was surely the first time that the Paris house had produced an example of the *nath*'.[55]

The exchange of influence between Cartier and India came full circle when, in 1933, Jeanne Toussaint, one of the firm's stylistic innovators and an avid collector of Indian jewellery, almost overnight 'brought yellow gold, in India sacred to the Gods, back into vogue'.[56]

Tribal Jewellery

This catalogue concentrates on the gold jewellery of the Indian subcontinent, which is worn by preference by everyone who can afford it. Only where there is a religious prohibition against the wearing of gold ornaments, notably on the feet, is silver substituted (see p. 120). Passing fashion seems not to have altered the preeminence of gold over the centuries; gold ornaments may be more heavily jewelled or less, but the use of gold, apart from the short-lived vogue for platinum in the 1920s (see p. 47), has been constant. However, there are, of course, millions for whom gold is out of reach. This section shows that lack of precious materials has never inhibited the wearing of jewellery and that poverty and even lack of technical skill has not prevented the creation of innovative and striking forms.

A small group of tribal jewellery from the Naga Hills has, therefore, been chosen to illustrate this theme. The area of Eastern Assam bordering Burma has, for an unknown period of time, been the home of tribal groups whose origins are equally unknown. They are migrants, and preserve the memory of their migration, but from where exactly they came is a matter for speculation. Even the name 'Naga' is a mystery, but may mean 'naked people'. Despite having scant regard for clothing, their personal adornment, from warrior headdresses to flower jewellery, seems always to have been important.

The materials used for their jewellery are necessarily simple: carnelian, rock crystal, shells, beads, flowers, blue jay feathers and animal hair dyed red are all used. Some ornaments are made from heavily cast brass and may serve a dual function; if need be they can be slipped off the arm to become formidable weapons (fig. 20). Certain ornaments are worn only by particular sections of a given tribe. Among the Eastern Rengami Nagas, for instance, only the men wear flowers in their ears, red being the favourite colour.[57] The Angami Naga men wear green fern or other foliage in their hair knots.

The Nagas were head-hunters, and both the ritual of a particular group and the ornaments worn by men who had taken heads are intimately connected with this. The necklet (no. 127), for instance, would have been worn only by a head-hunter,

Fig. 20 (left)
A Kabrii boy.
Detail from a photograph taken in 1902
Royal Anthropological Institute: no. 382

Fig. 21 (right)
Study of a Muslim fakir.
Toned gelatin silver print photograph
Photographer unknown
Madras; c. 1920–30
V&A: Indian Department

The Nagas were head-hunters, and both the ritual of a particular group and the ornaments worn by men who had taken heads are intimately connected with this. The necklet (no. 127), for instance, would have been worn only by a head-hunter, and Jean-Paul Barbier notes that the swirling, incised motifs on some of the brass armlets are also those permitted only on head-hunters' jewellery.[58]

In terms of colour, perhaps the most beautiful piece of 'jewellery' in the catalogue is the beetle necklace (no. 126) which was worn by a young man of the Zemi Naga tribe. The radiant iridescence of the peacock blue and vibrant green is unsurpassed by anything made by man. The brass armlets (no. 129) which were worn by women of different tribes are roughly cast and crudely incised but are strikingly imaginative both in their abstraction and in the way in which they would have been worn, with the recurving ends pointing backwards.

The Muslim fakir (fig. 21) comes from a tradition that could not be more different; he uses ornaments again of the poorest type but in a way which is not concerned with beauty of effect. All his possessions are to be seen in the photograph, from the coins and cowrie shells worn in his hair, to the metal crutch on which he leans in meditation. The heavy, cast metal bangles are the identifying mark of his sect; unfortunately, the caption on the back of the photograph does not identify it but gives the mysterious information that he is 'carrying 225lb.'

Footnotes

1. R.H. Major (ed.), *India in the Fifteenth Century, Being a Collection of Narratives of Voyages to India*, London, 1857, p. 26.

2. G.P. Badger (ed.), *The Travels of Ludovico de Varthema in Egypt, Syria, Arabia Deserta and Arabia Felix, in Persia, India and Ethiopia*, AD *1503 to 1508*, London, Hakluyt Society, 1863, p. 118.

3. *Ibid.*, p. 127.

4. Mansel Longworth Dames (trs.), *The Book of Duarte Barbosa. An Account of the Countries Bordering on the Indian Ocean and Their Inhabitants, Written by Duarte Barbosa, and Completed About the Year 1518* AD London 1918, vol. II, p. 19.

5. Where the Deccan is concerned, information is even scarcer. No Sultanate period jewellery has survived, and there are far fewer paintings to show what the jewellery worn looked like. Broadly speaking, though there are ornaments of a specifically local type, dependence on Iranian forms is strong, reflecting the cultural sympathy between Iran and the Deccan, as well as the political involvement of Iranians at the different courts. With the rise of the Mughal empire, Mughal forms became widely used and with the capitulation of the Sultanates in the late seventeenth century, 'Mughalisation' becomes almost total.

6. William Foster (ed.), *Early Travels in India,* Oxford, 1921, p.103. Although Hawkins reached the court during Jahangir's reign, the vast quantities of jewelled objects and precious raw materials could not conceivably all have been collected after Akbar's death. The description must, therefore, also stand for Akbar's reign.

7. *Ibid.*, p.111. The 'rottie' meant *rati*, the seed of *Abrus precatorius,* used as a jewellers' weight.

8. R. P. Kangle (trs.), *The Kauṭilya Arthaśāstra, part II,* (second edition, Bombay, 1972, p. 98.)

9. Col. H. S. Jarrett (trs.), *The A'in-i Akbari*, vol. III, reprint edition, Delhi, 1978, p. 343.

10. N. B. Divatia, 'The Nose-ring as an Indian Ornament,' *Journal of the Asiatic Society of Bengal*, 1923, N.S., vol. XIX, Calcutta, 1924, pp. 67-70; K. N. Chatterjee 'The Use of Nose Ornaments in India,' *ibid.*, vol. XXII, Calcutta, 1929, pp. 287-95; cf. P.K. Gode 'The Antiquity of the Hindoo Nose Ornament called "Nath" ', *Studies in Cultural History*, vol. II, Poona, 1960, pp. 142-59.

11. Gode, *ibid.*, p. 147.

12. Longworth Dames, *ibid.*, p. 207.

13. Jarrett, *ibid.*, pp. 345 ff.

14. *Ibid.*, p. 344.

15. The ceremonial weighing of the emperor took place twice a year. He was weighed against various classes of articles, ranging from gold and silver to

grain, which were then, in theory, to be distributed amongst the poor. The princes, sons and grandsons of the emperor were weighed once a year.

16. William Foster (ed.), *The Embassy of Sir Thomas Roe to the Court of the Great Mogul, 1615-1619,* Kraus reprint edition, Nendeln, 1967.

17. Alexander Rogers and Henry Beveridge, *The Tūzūk-i-Jahāngīrī or Memoirs of Jahangir,* London, 1909, vol. I, p. 167.

18. *Ibid.,* vol. II, p. 80.

19. Archibald Constable, *Travels in the Mogul Empire AD 1656-1668,* London, 1891, p. 268.

20. See Stronge, 1986, p. 315.

21. Stronge, *loc. cit.*

22. See Meene and Tushingham, 1971.

23. See Ivanov, 1984, *passim.*

24. Robert Skelton *et al., Treasures from India, The Clive Collection at Powis Castle,* London, 1987, no. 89.

25. Rai Krishnadasa, 1971, p. 30.

26. Christie's (London), *Islamic, Indian, and South-east Asian manuscripts, miniatures and works of art,* Tuesday 24 November 1987, lot 247.

27. Ivanov, 1984, especially no. 99, pl. 163, no. 98, pl. 161.

28. *The Indian Heritage,* no. 311

29. Hendley, vol. XII, p. 22.

30. See Bibliography.

31. Havell, 1892, pl. 35.

32. R. Nagaswamy, *The Art of Tamilnadu,* State Department of Archaeology, Government of Tamilnadu, 1972, fig. 33.

33. *Ibid.,* fig. 32.

34. *Ibid.,* fig. 31.

35. Tagore, vol. I, p. 459.

36. I am greatly indebted to Miss Judy Rudoe for drawing my attention to this catalogue. The daughter of Charles Cornwallis, Governor-General of India who led the 1792 campaign against Tipu, married the third Baron Braybrooke; the ring was, presumably, part of the booty taken and divided as 'prize'.

37. Such as the swords at Windsor and Powis Castle.

38. R. Nagaswamy, 'Mughal cultural influence in the Setupáti murals in the Ramalinga Vilasam at Ramnad' in Robert Skelton *et al.(eds.), Facets of Indian Art,* London, 1986, pp. 203-10.

39. *Ibid.* fig. 12.

40. Wilkinson, 1987.

41. *Ibid.,* p. 276.

42. Parks, 1850, p. 12.

43. See Dora Jane Janson, *From Slave to Siren. The Victorian Woman and her Jewelry from Neoclassic to Art Nouveau,* Duke University Museum of Art, Durham, North Carolina, 1971, p. 44, no. 80.

44. See O'Day, 1974, pl. 41; see also Munn, 1987, fig. 1.

45. See Gere, 1972, p. 196-99.

46. Haweis, 1878, p. 81.

47. Eastlake, 1868, p. 241.

48. Gere, 1972, p. 145.

49. *Ibid.,* p. 186.

50. Nadelhofer, 1984, p. 82.

51. *Ibid.,* p. 86.

52. *Ibid.,* p. 45.

53. *Ibid.,* p. 158.

54. *Ibid.,* p. 159.

55. *Ibid.,* p. 180.

56. *Ibid.,* p. 182.

57. J. P. Mills, *The Rangma Nagas,* London, 1977, p. 31.

58. Barbier, 1982, pl. 25.

Turban Jewels

37
Turban jewels (*jīgha* and *sarpati*)
Enamelled gold set with diamonds, rubies, emeralds, a sapphire, and a pendent pearl
Bengal (Murshidabad); c. 1755
Jīgha H 16.9 cm W 6.1 cm; *sarpati* W 10.6 cm H 3.6 cm (excl. pearl)
IS 3-1982

These jewels were presented to Admiral Charles Watson by the Nawab of Bengal on 26 July 1757, following the battle of Plassey. They remained in the possession of the Townley family, the descendants of the Admiral, until 1982 when the Museum bought them at auction and are the only documented Murshidabad jewels known so far. Following the capture of Calcutta by Siraj ad-Daula, the British felt their trading interests in Bengal to be under severe threat. It was, therefore, decided that the Nawab should be deposed in favour of one who would be more amenable to British designs. Robert Clive directed the operation, Watson commanded the fleet, and the chosen replacement was Mir Ja'far ʿAli Khan. The climax came with the Battle of Plassey. Though barely significant militarily

37 (front)

37 (back)

(Mir Ja'far caused most of Siraj ad-Daula's troops to retreat at a crucial point, leading to the inevitable capitulation to the British), the battle changed the history of the subcontinent by paving the way for the British 'Raj'.

Mir Ja'far being safely installed, the inevitable presents were made to the key figures. Edward Ives, who was involved in the campaign, noted that on 26 July 1757 the new Nawab sent presents, after the custom of the country, to the Admiral. These included 'a rose and plume composed of diamonds, rubies, sapphires and emeralds, which though not of great value, made a pompous appearance' (Edward Ives, *A Voyage from India in the Year 1754,*London, 1773, p. 154). These appear in a painting of Watson and his son, where his son wears Indian dress and has the jewels in his turban (see Sotheby & Co. p. 46 – see below).

The jewels are typical of the Murshidabad court fashion at the time. A painting of ᶜAliverdi Khan of c. 1750–55 (fig.11) shows the Nawab with his young grandson Siraj ad-Daula; both wear turban jewels of exactly the same form.

Clive appears also to have been given a similar *jīgha*: the 1987 Geneva exhibition of Mughal jewellery shows a piece which is said to have come from his collection and relates closely to that shown here (Markevitz, 1987, pp. 74–5). His accounts show that he owned several jewelled turban ornaments.

PUBLISHED
Sotheby & Co., *Catalogue of Jewels for the Collector,* Thursday 22 April, 1982, lot 274.
Stronge, 1985.
Welch, 1985, cat. 183.
Stronge, 1986, figs. 9 and 10.

38 (back)

38
Turban ornament *(jīgha)*
Gold set with rubies, diamonds, emeralds and pale beryls enamelled in translucent green on the stem
Rajasthan?; early 18th century
H 16.8 cm W 5.8 cm
IM 240-1923

Sprays of flowers are commonplace in Mughal art but it is extremely rare to find a turban jewel reproducing the characteristic border motif of countless textiles, miniatures and metal artefacts. It is part of an important group of aigrettes bought by the V&A in 1922 and 1923 from a Mr Talyarkhan, who purchased them from the Maharajah of Jaipur. The vendor seems to have suggested that this was an imperial Mughal piece which had been presented to Jaipur, but the similarity in style between it and the unusual *jīgha* worn by the Mewar Maharana Bhim Singh (fig.12) may indicate that it was a Rajput form.

PUBLISHED
The Indian Heritage, cat. 308.
Stronge, 1982, p. 317.

38 (front)

39
Incomplete turban ornament
Enamelled gold backed with lac
Possibly Jaipur; c.1750
H 17.3 cm W 5 cm
IM 47-1922

The jewelled front of this has been removed, exposing the lac layer. Like no. 38 purchased from Jaipur, it was said to have been one of the products of Jaipur itself. It is similar in form to the Murshidabad *jīgha* and has a close decorative similarity in its use of poppy motifs (deriving ultimately from Jahangir's tomb at Lahore of 1627). However, the skills of the Jaipur enameller far surpassed those of his Murshidabad counterpart.

40
Turban ornament (*jīgha*)
Enamelled gold
Mughal (or Jaipur); 18th century
H 12 cm W 3.6 cm
IM 44-1922

This jewel demonstrates the technique of *basse taille* where the gold is chased with a design which can be seen through the translucent enamel. The technique is found with reasonable frequency in Mughal jewellery, but is rarely seen on such a scale, usually being confined to small details (e.g. the stem of no. 38).

41
Turban jewel (*jīgha*)
Enamelled gold set with rubies
Possibly Jaipur; early 18th century
H 7.9 cm W 3 cm
IM 45-1922

This was also part of the Jaipur treasury (see no. 38) and was said on acquisition to date from the first half of the eighteenth century. It is notable for the excellence of its enamelling which does not show a trace of 'flooding'. It has a holder for a long feathered plume at the back.

39 41 40

Turban Jewels · 55

42
Turban ornament (*jīgha*)
Enamelled gold set with emeralds and diamonds and with pendent pearls and emeralds
Udaipur, Rajasthan; 19th century
H 11 cm W 13.5 cm
Lent by Gracious Permission of Her Majesty the Queen

This was presented by the Maharana of Udaipur to the Prince of Wales on his tour of India of 1875–6. Probably dating from the nineteenth century, it is in a traditional style which develops out of the early eighteenth-century example seen above (no. 38). The stones are of impressive size and many are faceted; in Indian jewellery this is usually only done to the larger stones and, even then, many are simply cut *en cabochon* (cf. no. 37, the large sapphire). Some of these stones, such as the emerald at the centre of the section on the right which is bored for stringing, have served other purposes in the past. This is a common practice; the best stones in a treasury would be reset as fashions, or the whim of the ruler, changed.

PUBLISHED
Catalogue of the Collection of Indian Art ... at Marlborough House, London, 1891, no. 51, p. 4 and fig. facing p. 2.

56 · Jewellery of the Mughal Period

43
Turban ornament *(jīgha)*
Enamelled gold
Jaipur; first half of 19th century
H 12 cm W 13 cm
IM 241-1923

This, the last of the group from the Jaipur treasury, is enamelled in colours which are usually thought of as the typical Jaipur palette: a red, white, blue and green mixture with touches of opaque powder blue and yellow. It may originally have had pearls in the outer border of floral calyxes.

Ornaments for the Head

44
Forehead ornament *(tikka)*
Gold set with diamonds and rubies, enamelled on the back, and with baroque pendant pearls
N. India; 18th century (the chain European)
H 4.3 cm (7.3 inc. pendent pearls) W 2.6 cm
IS 1-1976
Given by Mrs Jean Buchanan Scott

This would originally have had a strand of seed pearls with which to attach it to the hair. A closely comparable example is illustrated in the Gentil album of 1774 (fig. 6).

44

45
Hair ornament
Gold, set with turquoise on one side and rubies on the other, with strings of pearls and pearl pendants tipped with green glass
Delhi; c. 1850
H 14.5 cm
03181 IS

PUBLISHED
Hendley, vol. XII, part I, pl. 5, no. 22.

45 (back)   *Overleaf:* 45 (front)

Ornaments for the Head · 59

46
Hair ornament
Gold set with rubies, emeralds and diamonds, and with strings of pearls and red glass beads
Northern India, possibly Oudh; mid-19th century
L coiled pendants 23 cm
03209 IS

This hair ornament was an exhibition piece acquired by the Indian Museum in 1855. It would have been worn with the long coils, terminating in serpent heads, framing the face and the strings of pearls with pendants fanning out over the forehead. Fanny Parks, in 1828, described the coiffure of the young wife of the King of Oudh: 'I never saw anyone so lovely ... her hair was literally strewed with pearls, which hung down upon her neck in long single strings, terminating in large pearls, which mixed with and hung as low as her hair, which was curled on each side of her head in long ringlets, like Charles the Second's beauties' (Parks, 1850, vol. 1 p. 88).

It is conceivable that this hair ornament is a jewelled stylisation of the ringlets. Mrs Haque, in her book on Bangladesh jewellery, calls this ornament *jhapta* (see below).

PUBLISHED
Hendley, vol. XII, fig. 740.
Arts of Bengal, 1979, cat. 211.
Haque, 1984, fig. 65.

◀ 45 (front)

60 · Jewellery of the Mughal Period

47
Forehead ornament
Gold set with foiled rock crystal and pearls
Panjab (Gujranwala); c. 1850
H 9 cm W 23.2 cm
03133 IS

Unusually for jewellery from the north of the subcontinent, this ornament (which would be worn along the hair line with the pendant resting on the forehead) is not enamelled on the back. It was acquired by the Indian Museum in 1855, presumably from the Paris exhibition, and was made in the birthplace of the Lion of the Panjab, Ranjit Singh (see no. 64). Maclagan, 1890, commented that while Delhi and Amritsar would supply jewellery in almost any style, the work of Gujranwala (like that of Lahore and Peshawar) had 'a celebrity of a very local character' (p. 12).

48
Forehead ornament
Gold and gilt metal set with rubies, emeralds and pearls
Probably Madras; 19th century
W 26.6 cm H 4.3 cm
42-1893 IS

This was bought from Messrs Proctor & Co's Indian Art Gallery at 428 Oxford Street, in 1893. Their invoices advertise that they were 'Indian Jewellers and Importers of Works of Art from Bombay, Madras, Bengal, Agra, Delhi, etc.'.

PUBLISHED
Hendley, vol XII, fig. 639.

49
Hair ornament (*sīsphūl*)
Gold, worked in repoussé, backed with silver and filled with lac
Bangalore; probably c. 1880
DIAM. 11.5 cm
1861-1883 IS

This ornament, its minute detail meticulously worked and its central projecting section separately made and soldered in, is characteristically south Indian. It symbolises the sun god, Surya, and depicts the god Vishnu at the centre, lying on the serpent Ananta whose multiple heads fan out over him, his consorts (in this south Indian form) Shridevi and Bhudevi on either side. The south Indian *ayah* in the Reynolds painting (fig. 18) wears a smaller version of this type of ornament, probably also with the same motifs as it has a projection at the top which could be the heads of Ananta; a lady in the album of c. 1830 also wears one on the back of her head (fig. 13). On the back, in English, is the information that the ornament cost 80 rupees, the gold accounting for 75 rupees, and the silver back and lac 5 rupees. It was bought for the South Kensington Museum by Caspar Purdon Clarke for £9 on his Indian tour of 1881-2.

50
Hair ornaments
Gold worked in repoussé, chased, filled with lac and backed with silver
Poona; c. 1880
Above left (1877): DIAM. 5.9 cm H 6.6 cm; above right (1876): W 4.2 cm H 4.7 cm; below (1879): W 2.7 cm
1876, 1877 and 1879-1883 IS

Each ornament is worked in thin sheet gold which is a framed by a gold ring and filled with lac, the frame then being crimped over a silver back (missing on 1877). The motifs are lotuses and birds; 1876 combines birds with a multi-headed, coiled serpent with a crescent moon beneath representing the moon deity (*candra purai*); the disc represents the sun god (*surya purai*).

PUBLISHED
Hendley, vol. XII, figs. 670, 671, 684.

50

51

51
Hair ornament
Gold, worked in repoussé, chased and backed with gold
Bombay; probably c. 1880
H 4.8 cm W 4.3 cm
1985-1883 IS

The ornament is hollow; its cobra hood with multiple heads coils over a sinuously-tailed peacock flanked by less flamboyant versions. The flowerheads above the cobras are pierced and were perhaps intended to hold pearls. Along each side are attachment rings.

Ornaments for the Head · 63

52
Pair of ear ornaments *(karanphūl)*
Enamelled gold, and silver, set with quartz, with seed pearls, blue glass beads and red glass pendants
Delhi; c. 1850
H 7 cm DIAM. rosette 3.3 cm
03305 IS

53
Pair of ear ornaments
Gold filigree and silver set with diamonds; pendants of pearls, green glass and emeralds, strands of pearls and rubies
Varanasi (Benares); c. 1850
H 16.5 cm
03254 IS

The considerable weight of these ornaments is only partly supported by the hook which passes through the ear; the strands of pearls would be looped up and the twisted gold tie threaded into the hair. European influence shows itself in the filigree borders.

53

54
Ear ornament *(kanphatā)*
Chased and pierced gold with 'cut work',
pendants of filigree and sheet gold strips
Calcutta; c. 1870
H 19.3 cm
995-1872

This style of 'cut-work' almost certainly derives from European cut-steel jewellery of the late eighteenth century, produced in England notably at Woodstock near Oxford and by Matthew Boulton at his Soho, Birmingham, factory, and enjoying considerable popularity in France (see Anne Clifford, *Cut Steel and Berlin Iron Jewellery*, London, 1971). The fashion continued into the nineteenth century but lost its appeal in about 1850. The Indian jewellers, apart from using a different material, also used different techniques, suggesting that the models came from jewellers' catalogues rather than actual examples. Early European cut steel would have the faceted studs riveted individually onto a steel plate; later they were stamped in strips. Indian pieces were lighter, as would be expected from the costly and more malleable nature of gold. The studs were either soldered individually onto an openwork wire frame (as here) or stamped out and then pierced between each stud (no. 55). The sharply-reflecting surfaces on some pieces are softened by a coating of tamarind juice which gives a subtle red sheen. The main section of this ornament clips on to the outer curve of the ear.

PUBLISHED
Hendley, vol XII, fig. 795.
Arts of Bengal, 1979, cat. 214.
cf. Haque, 1985, fig. 80.

55
Pair of earrings
Gold 'cut work' studs set onto plain or twisted wire, with applied small flat discs
Calcutta; c. 1850
H 6 cm W 4.5 cm
03249 IS

PUBLISHED
Hendley, vol. XII, fig. 747.

56 (one only illustrated)
Pair of ear-drops *(karanphūl)*
Gold filigree with pendent sheet gold strips
Mirzapur; c. 1850
H 6 cm
03303 IS

These were acquired by the Indian Museum in 1855, probably from the Paris Exposition Universelle of that year.

Each section has a filigree frame onto which are soldered gold granules, or circular cushions of spiralling wire surmounted by a slightly larger granule. Each pendent 'bell' has small strips of thin sheet gold attached to it which tremble with the slightest movement, causing light to flicker across them.

66 · Jewellery of the Mughal Period

57
Ear pendant
Gold with applied wire, granulation and stamped motifs
Madras; c. 1885
H 9.5 cm W 2.6 cm
153-1886 IS

This pendant came from the London Colonial and Indian Exhibition of 1886. The richly textured surface of the upper crescent is produced by applying alternate bands of twisted wires and granulation, the grains either being arranged in a single row or in clusters of four, with an additional one on top. On the outside are circles of coiled wires with applied grains. The long pendant, held by a coiled and looped wire, is simpler but no less painstakingly crafted, with its applied plaited wire borders, and wire-and-granule flowers.

58
Pair of ear ornaments (*nāgavadura*)
Gold with applied stamped motifs, gold wires and granulation
Vellore, Madras; c. 1880
H 2.8 cm DIAM. ring base 1.1 cm
1939-1883 IS

Though these ear ornaments are very obviously stylised cobras or *nagas*, the upper projecting section is the head of a semi-abstract animal (bat?) with long ears and fangs. It thus relates to the group of ear ornaments with bizarre animal and bird heads described below (no. 59). Another shared feature is the use of geometric motifs. This pair would have been worn with five other ornaments on each ear by *sudra* women (Havell, 1892, p. 32 and pl. 35, figs. 1–6). Brass imitations were substituted if gold was too expensive.

59
Ear ornament
Hollow gold, with applied geometric elements
Tamilnadu; 20th century
H 4.8 cm W (max.) 5.7 cm
IS 5-1986

This ear ornament would be worn with one or two others of similar size and weight, thus dragging down and distending the lobe to an extraordinary degree (see fig. 25). The form is also produced in silver (Welch, 1986, cat. 70, p. 115).

Ornaments for the Head · 67

60
Nose ring (nāth)
Gilt metal set with a pearl and with applied wire and granulation
India; 19th century (acquired before 1884)
H 6 cm   W 5.6 cm
Lent by the Pitt Rivers Museum, Oxford:
PR Coll. black 60/1631

The nose ring is usually worn by married women and, though now seen as quintessentially Indian, seems to have been introduced into the subcontinent from abroad (see p. 29).

61
Nose pendant (bulāq)
Gilt metal set with turquoise
Sultanpur, Kulu; probably c. 1880
H 9.1 cm
1116-1883 IS

This is a modest example of Kulu nose pendants which may reach extravagant proportions and require a complex system of pulley-like supports for their weight (see Untracht, 1982, p. 350). Maclagan, 1890, notes that two forms of nose ornament were worn in Kulu, usually of gold. This type would have been worn by married or unmarried women (though never by widows), while the larger bālū was the mark of a married woman (p. 35).

Pendants and Necklaces

62
Pendant *(ta'vīz)*
White nephrite jade in a pierced gold frame, set with rubies and emeralds in gold and with a pendent emerald, the back inscribed and set with a ruby in gold
Mughal; first half of 17th century
H 5.7 cm W 5 cm
02535 IS

This came from the collection of Colonel Charles Seton Guthrie who also owned the famous nephrite drinking cup of Shah Jahan in the Victoria and Albert Museum. The palmette at the centre relates to those found in the Iranian-influenced decorative arts of the late sixteenth and early seventeenth centuries, rather than to the period of Shah Jahan when floral decoration became more naturalistic. The detail is painstaking, with the eyes of the birds being minute emeralds set in gold. The back is inscribed with a Koranic verse.

The amulet, which is bored along the top edge, would have been the central pendant to a necklace. A *ta'vīz* in the Bharat Kala Bhavan with almost exactly the same profile, though differing at the top, is dated 1051 AH/1640 AD (Morley, 1971, fig. 244). A later example of the same type is dated 1071 AH/1660 AD and is in the Chester Beatty Library, Dublin (David James, 'Islamic Hardstone Carving', *Kunst und Antiquitäten*, II/81, fig. 1).

Pendants and Necklaces · 69

63 (back) ▶

(63 front)

63
Pendant
Enamelled gold, set with rubies and a diamond on the front, and with green glass imitating emeralds
Mughal; 18th century
H 3.7 cm W 3 cm
BM: OA + 14178

This pendant, with its carefully shaped, flat-set rubies, and green glass imitating emeralds, is worked in a style which goes back to the late sixteenth century (see no. 93) The gemstones are used almost like mosaics, set into chased depressions and separated by gold left in slight relief to delineate the pattern. The residual areas are then engraved with flowers and foliage. The back is beautifully enamelled in a rhythmic portrayal of a bird amongst flowers, using the standard Mughal palette of white, red and green, though with touches of opaque yellow and blue.

PUBLISHED
Tait, 1986, p. 174, fig. 395.

64
Order of merit
Enamelled gold set with emeralds and a miniature portrait of Ranjit Singh under rock crystal
Lahore; 1837–9
H 9.1 cm W 4.8 cm
IS 92-1981

This Order of Merit seems to have been introduced by Ranjit Singh in direct emulation of the Légion d'Honneur worn by one of his foreign military commanders, General Allard (see Henry Edward Fane, *Five Years in India*, London, 1842, vol. 1, p. 181). The general may be seen in a painting of 1838 in S.C. Welch, *Room for Wonder*, New York, 1978, no. 55. This example came from the collection of Ranjit Singh's son, Dalip Singh.

PUBLISHED
Christie's, London, *Objects of Vertu*, Tuesday, 24 February, 1981, no. 25.
See also Mohan Singh, 'Medals of Maharaja Ranjit Singh' in *Maharaja Ranjit Singh as Patron of the Arts*, Marg Publications, Bombay, 1981, pp. 125–30.

65
Necklace
Enamelled gold and silver pendant set with rubies, emeralds, natural white sapphires and rock crystal, strands of pearls and emerald with two rubies
North India; 19th century
L 28 cm
41-1873
Given by Major N. G. Davies

Necklaces like this could have been made at almost any time in the eighteenth and nineteenth centuries. However, the crowded effect of the red, white, blue and green motifs on the back of the pendant suggests nineteenth-century decadence when compared with the unconstricted designs of eighteenth-century pieces.

Pendants and Necklaces · 73

▲ 66 (back)

◀ 66 (front)

66
Necklace
Enamelled gold plaques and pendants, some set with pendent pearls and green glass beads; the strands of pearls terminate in emerald and ruby beads
North India; 19th century
L 29 cm
03183 IS

Each of the large central pendants is enamelled with slightly different motifs using the same red, white and green palette, highlighted with touches of pale blue. The plaques which secure the strings of pearls are enamelled in an unusual combination of opaque yellow and white flowers with lime green leaves on a translucent red ground.

74 · Jewellery of the Mughal Period

Pendants and Necklaces · 75

67
Necklet
Enamelled gold, set with diamonds and pearls, with pendent pearls and emeralds
North India; c. 1850
DIAM 18.5 cm W 17 cm
03202 IS

This was acquired by the Indian Museum in 1855.

◂ 67 (back)

67 (front)

68
Necklace
Enamelled gold set with diamonds, with strands of pearls, rubies and green glass
North India; c. 1850
L 27 cm
03177 IS

Like the preceding necklet, this was acquired by the Indian Museum in 1855; both were almost certainly exhibition pieces.

PUBLISHED
Hendley, vol. XII, fig. 734.

76 · *Jewellery of the Mughal Period*

69
Marriage necklace *(thālī)*
Gold beads and pendant on black thread, the gold worked in repoussé or stamped, with applied wire decoration and cut work panels, inscribed on the back
Tamilnadu, south India; late 19th century
Pendant H 12.5 cm   W 6.4 cm
IS 90-1987

The imposing pendant of this necklace is adorned with the images of the god Shiva and his consort Parvati seated on Nandi, the sacred bull, before a temple, all worked in repoussé which is pierced in places to reveal the gleam of a red foil backing. Above this, contrasting strongly both in its flatness and in the delicate curving of its cut tracery, is an applied panel depicting a deer dancing on its hind legs between birds of paradise taking flight. A second panel, beneath the repoussé panel, has similar birds arranged on a formal scrolling ground with a central palmette.

69 (detail of pendant) ▶

70
Marriage necklace *(thālī)*
Stamped and chased, lac-filled pendants on black thread
Madura; 19th century
L (approx) 38 cm (doubled); L cylindrical pendants 6.9 cm and 7.2 cm
1869-1883 IS

A necklace of this type can be seen on the small girl in fig. 17. The cylindrical pendants, probably deriving ultimately from Iranian forms, are called *thayittu*; Havell commented that these were intended to contain small pieces of paper inscribed with Sanskrit mantras, 'but goldsmiths now often lose sight of the original intention of the *thayittu* and simply fill it with lac'. (Havell, 1892, p. 34). The pendants are auspicious emblems; fruits and vegetables signifying abundance, or miniature representations of temple pinnacles. This was acquired by Caspar Purdon Clarke on his purchasing tour of India of 1881–2, and was said to be from Madura.

PUBLISHED
Hendley, vol. XII, fig. 682.

◀ 70

71

71
Marriage necklace *(thālī)*
Sheet gold with applied wires and stamped motifs imitating granulation; the red silk ties with beads with twisted grooves
Travancore or Malabar; c. 1850
L 30 cm
03061 IS

Havell includes a similar necklace in his photographs of jewellery from the western littoral of southern India which, he notes, was very different in character to that worn in the east (Havell, 1894, p. 70). This was acquired by the Indian Museum in 1855.

PUBLISHED
Hendley, vol. XII, fig. 634.

80 · *Jewellery of the Mughal Period*

72

72
Necklace
Gilt metal beads and pendants on red silk
Vellore, south India; c. 1880
L 37.3 cm
1981-1883 IS

Havell shows a necklace with similar beads which he notes is worn by low castes everywhere in southern India (Havell, 1892, p. 30). This was acquired by Caspar Purdon Clarke on his tour of India in 1881–2.

73
Filigree necklace
Gold wire with stamped florets and applied flat discs and hemispheres
Calicut; c. 1850
L (approx) 33.5 cm W (approx) 34 cm
124-1852

This extremely fine necklace was bought from the 1851 Great Exhibition as 'modern' work from Calicut. It is an exhibition piece in the best sense, an impressive example of the craftsman's skills, though using, by Indian standards, mass production techniques in the stamping of some of the motifs.

PUBLISHED
Havell, 1894, pl. 19A.

73 ▶

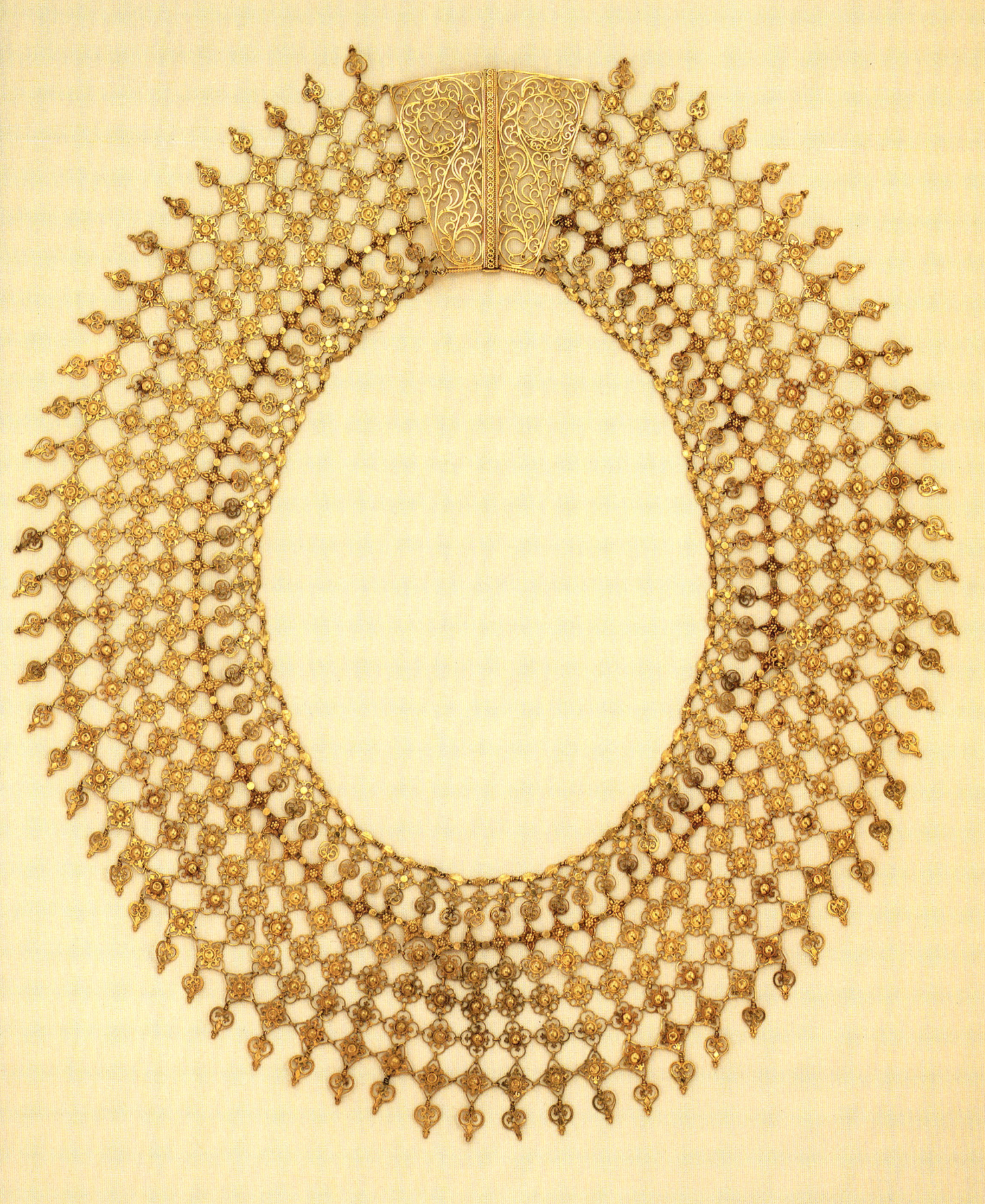

82 · *Jewellery of the Mughal Period*

74
Necklace
Beads of gold wire, with applied granulation and minute flat discs, with gold links
Calcutta; c. 1850
03299 IS

Each of the 144 beads on this necklace has three levels, a central rosette of flat wires and triangular groups of granules at the apex of each alternate petal. Overlaid on this, at front and back, is another rosette with minute flattened discs on the tips of the petals.

75
Necklace
Interlinked gold pendants on doubled gold chain
Calicut; c. 1850
L 58 cm
1805-1852

Each pendant is stamped out from a flat sheet of gold with applied twisted wires and granulation at the front. The pendants interlink by means of rings running through their four loops. The lower edge of the necklace has pendent filigree vases, many now missing.

76
Necklace
Tiger-claws set in engraved gold and linked by chains, suspended from a 'snake' chain
India; c. 1865
L 43.5 cm
594-1868 IS

The necklace, its ten tiger-claws graded in size, was purchased by the South Kensington Museum from the 1867 Paris Exposition Universelle where it was described as 'modern' work.

Tigers' claws are regarded as charms against evil; Fanny Parks (1850, p. 12) commented: 'If you kill a tiger, the servants steal his claws as quickly as possible to send to their wives to make into charms, which both women and children wear around their necks. They arrest the evil eye and keep off maladies'. When she gave tiger-claws to her friend, the grand-daughter of the Maharani of Scindia, this lady followed the illustrious example of the Mughal emperor Akbar and had them mounted in gold for her horse to wear (see V&A *Akbarnama*: IS 2-1896 33/117). Mrs Parks had a tiger-claw charm made in silver in the Fatehgarh bazaar, which copied that worn by the wife of one of her Muslim servants, and which is illustrated in her book.

Tiger-claw jewellery was also made for the British, no doubt as an exotic souvenir of their life in India; an elaborate parure is illustrated in Margaret Flower's book on Victorian jewellery (Flower, 1967, fig. 53).

77
Brooch and pendant
Tiger-claws set in sheet gold worked in repoussé
Travancore; c. 1870
H brooch 7.7 cm W 10.2 cm; H pendant 5.7 cm
Lent by Gracious Permission of Her Majesty the Queen

Tiger-claw jewellery has a long history in Hindu India, being seen for example on a twelfth-century image of Subrahmanya (see Haque, 1984, fig. 5); Subrahmanya is one of the names of Karttikeya, the god of war. This brooch and pendant were presented by the Maharaja of Travancore to the Prince of Wales on his Indian tour of 1875-6. The goddess Lakshmi, being lustrated by elephants, is depicted on the brooch.

PUBLISHED
Catalogue of the Collection of Indian Arts and Objects of Art ... at Marlborough House, 1891, no. 214, p. 14.

86 · *Jewellery of the Mughal Period*

78
Necklace
Gold, pavé-set with seed pearls and turquoises, the heads with ruby eyes and enamelled details
Bengal; c. 1850
L 34 cm
03228 IS

This necklace, with its chain of interlocking scales, is an adaption of the serpent jewellery which was especially popular in the early Victorian period. A European serpent necklace or bracelet would usually fasten by looping the articulated scaly body over the head (see O'Day, 1974, pl. 3 for an 1830s example).

On this piece, however, the scales terminate in two quite incongruous wolf-heads. These snarl at each other over three spheres covered with pavé-set turquoises and pearls, another feature borrowed from early Victorian jewellery. The symmetry of the heads is perhaps an echo of the paired *makaras* found on the enamelled armlets of Rajasthan (no. 85)

Pendants and Necklaces · 87

79
Two lockets
Enamelled gold set with diamonds
Jaipur; c. 1875
H 3.5 cm and 3.1 cm W 2.5 cm and 2.4 cm
IM 261-1927; IM 262-1927
Bequeathed by Lord Curzon of Kedlestone,
KG, GCSI, GCIE, DCL

Each locket has a rose-cut diamond at its centre, the other stones being roughly faceted, a rather unusual feature in Indian jewellery where small diamonds are, typically, flat-cut. The larger of the two lockets has translucent blue at the front, the smaller, a rather pale translucent green. The backs have similar motifs of red, green and blue birds and flowers on a white ground, on the larger contained within a quatrefoil frame and on the smaller within an oval.

80
Pendant *(latkan)*
Enamelled gold
Jaipur or Nathdvara; 19th century
H 6.4 cm W 7.1 cm
Lent by the Trustees of the Ashmolean Museum, Oxford: x300

This pendant would have been worn by pilgrims to the shrine of Shrinathji at Nathdvara in Rajasthan. *Srīnāthjī* appears on one side in a heart-shaped cartouche of translucent red enamel, surrounded by red, blue and green peacocks and flowers on a white ground. On the other the *vishnupada* is also seen, the feet adorned with symbols such as the *svastika,* the auspicious symbol known from ancient times in the subcontinent.

Arm Ornaments

81
Armlet *(bāzūband)*
Enamelled gold set with an emerald, yellow beryls (heliodor), pale emeralds and seed pearls
Mughal India; second half of the 18th century
W 9 cm
Lent by the Trustees of the British Museum: 1961 10-16.3
Louis C. G. Clarke Bequest

81 (front)

This armlet would have been tied on to the upper arm. It incorporates poppy motifs which have exact parallels on the Watson turban ornament of c.1750 (no. 37), with a powder-blue enclosing border found frequently on nineteenth-century jewellery. However, the broad swathes of red enamel on the petals of the large flowers framing the oval panel of the armlet and the four curling leaf sprays surrounding the six-petalled flower at the centre are both characteristic eighteenth-century decorative features.

81 (detail of back)

82
Pair of armlets
Enamelled gold, each set with foiled rock crystals, a spinel, coral, pearl and zircon
Mughal India; 18th century
L 30 cm
Lent by the Trustees of the Ashmolean Museum

These are set with coloured stones imitating the auspicious *navaratna* setting (see no. 83) and are listed in the Ashmolean Museum's 1886 *Anthropological Catalogue* as 'Old Ashmolean Collection, probably Tradescants'.' Although unlikely to be part of the Museum's founding collection (which consists largely of the objects collected by the Tradescants in the first half of the seventeenth century), the style of enamelling suggests that it is of the eighteenth century rather than later.

I am extremely grateful to Miss Monica Price, Assistant Curator of the Mineral Collections, University Museum, Oxford, for examing the stones on these armlets.

83
Pair of armlets (bāzūband)
Gold enamelled with translucent green and pale opaque turquoise and set with nine stones (*navaratna*) and diamonds
Delhi; c. 1850
W 6.3 cm H 3.1 cm
03199&a

These armlets were acquired by the Indian Museum in 1855, possibly from the Paris exhibition of that year. They would have been worn on the upper arm and are each set with the auspicious *navaratna*.

In the ancient Sanskrit texts dealing with precious and semi-precious stones, the *Ratnashastras*, there are nine stones which form the essential basis of study, though the list may be extended to include others (see Finot, 1896). These are divided into two sections, the *maharatnani*, or 'great' gems (diamond, pearl, ruby, sapphire and emerald) and the *uparatnani*. or 'lesser' gems (jacinth, topaz, cat's eye and coral). These, in turn, are linked to the planets: thus, the diamond (*vajra*) is linked with Venus, the ruby *(manikya)* with the sun, sapphire *(indranila)* with Saturn, and so on. In Indian jewellery these, or less precious stones of the same colour, are often found grouped together in the setting called *'navaratna'* (nine gems). Each planet may have a malign influence which can be averted by counterbalancing the stone which represents it in the correct way against its companions. Each stone may also bestow particular benefits on its wearer. The balancing of these stones in order to avert malevolent influences and to attract those which are benevolent may clearly become a complicated matter, though where cheaper substitutes are made, the effect is presumably more symbolic than otherwise. Generally, the ruby is at the centre, representing the sun, the giver of life.

The stones used here vary slightly on each armlet and include moonstone, pearl, ruby, turquoise, coral, aquamarine, diamond, orange sapphire, white sapphire and hessonite. One has nine rubies at its centre; the other has a diamond surrounded by what are probably white sapphires.

84
Armlet
Enamelled gold set with diamonds
Rajasthan (Dholpur?); c. 1850
DIAM 6.5 cm
119-1852

This armlet was acquired from London's Great Exhibition of 1851 as an example of 'modern' work from Dholpur. It is enamelled on the inside with lovebirds, parrots and flowers on a translucent red ground, which must have enchanted the careful observer at the exhibition. Though the traditional Mughal red, green and white predominate, there are unusual touches of opaque pale turquoise and yellow.

85
Bracelet
Enamelled gold set with diamonds
Rajasthan (Dholpur?); c. 1850
W each section 5 cm   H 2.4 cm
120-1852

This bracelet, in three hinged sections, is enamelled on the outside with the translucent royal blue popular in contemporary Victorian England. Like no. 84 it came from the Great Exhibition and was also described as modern work from Dholpur. The inside is enamelled with a scroll of red flowers and green leaves on a white ground, red and green parrots and pigeons pecking the leaves with translucent yellow or green beaks. A narrow band of opaque powder blue divides the front and back surfaces.

from the 1871 London Annual International Exhibition, illustrates a form which existed, unchanged, from at least 1600. It is seen in the 1621 manuscript of the *A'in-i Akbari* (British Library, London: Or 2169 f.3516) and is also illustrated in an album of drawings made by Robert Home, court artist to the King of Oudh, Ghazi ad-Din Haidar, who ruled from 1814-27 (V&A: E.1414-1943).

90

91
Pair of bangles
Gold worked in repoussé and chased, tinged with red and set with rubies
Madras; c. 1850
H 7.9 cm W 8.1 cm
03293 IS

Havell, (1892, p. 34 and pl. 41) notes that this type of bangle is worn by princes and rajahs and is bestowed by them on others as a mark of favour. It has two *makara* heads (see Glossary), with a stylised *rudraksha* bead, sacred to the god Shiva, between. A bracelet in the V&A's Jewellery Gallery has closely similar heads, though they are mounted on plaited gold wires. It was in the collection of Dante Gabriel Rossetti (1828-82) and was worn by the bride in his painting *The Bride, or The Beloved*, now in the Tate Gallery, executed in 1865-6 and retouched in 1873 (see Bury, 1982, p. 136, no. 5).

PUBLISHED
Hendley, vol. XII, fig 640.

92
Pair of bangles
Gold and gilt metal set with rubies
Madras; c. 1870
H 6.4 cm DIAM. 4.5 cm
1014 & a-1872

These were bought from the London Annual International Exhibition of 1872 for £25. Bangles with flat gold squares, set at an angle and projecting from the hoop, seem to have been very common at this period and are worn by many of the women in the V&A album of c. 1830 from Tanjore (see fig. 13).

Rings

93
Thumb ring
Engraved gold set with rubies and emeralds, enamelled in opaque colours on the inside
Mughal India; c. 1620-30
H 3.7 cm   DIAM. 3 cm
IM 207-1920

This ring is unequivocally a courtly piece. In shape and material, it relates closely to the thumb ring worn by Shah Jahan in the portrait of c. 1620 in the Metropolitan Museum of Art (illus. Welch *et al.*, 1987, cat. 55; the dust-jacket illustration gives a clear detail). In technique and quality, it is part of a small group of objects which date from the late sixteenth century to the mid-eighteenth century. The earliest of these, one of the finest examples of Mughal jewelled gold to have survived, is the V&A spoon (*The Indian Heritage,* cat. 322). Its jewelled palmettes, scrolls and birds set into engraved gold, the rubies and emeralds cut *en cabochon* or into thin slices and shaped to fit different parts of the design, characterise the group. Diamonds may be part of the composition, as with this spoon and a dagger of c. 1620 in the Kuwait National Museum (illus. Jenkins, 1983, p.126). The dagger is closely dateable by comparison with one worn by Shah Jahan in a portrait of c. 1618 (illus. *The Indian Heritage* cover), and has motifs in common with this ring. The colours and design of the enamel on the inside of the ring show an awareness of European Renaissance jewellery, the result either of European craftsmen at court, or of European jewels brought to the court for presentation to the emperor. The palette now seems to be extremely unusual, with its opaque pastels and black, but so little jewellery of the period has survived it is impossible to know whether or not it was commonplace (the *huqqa* ring in the Kuwait National Museum has opaque turquoise motifs against black on its rim; see Jenkins, 1983, p. 127).

The style continued into the eighteenth century (see no. 63) but is not so far known in nineteenth-century jewellery.

PUBLISHED
The Indian Heritage, cat. 303.
Welch, 1985, cat. 129.

94
Thumb ring
Enamelled gold set with diamonds
Northern India; 18th century, probably second half
H 3.9 cm   W 3 cm
02528 IS
From the Guthrie collection

A thumb ring of similar shape is illustrated on folio 33 of the album made for Gentil at Faizabad in 1774. The enamelled floral design on the inside of the ring was later copied by Robert Phillips for a necklace he exhibited at the 1867 Paris exhibition (no. 110).

PUBLISHED
The Indian Heritage cat. 306.

95
Seal ring
Chased gold set with an inscribed emerald
Ring probably S. India, 18th century; the seal
Iran, 18th century?
Seal H 0.9 cm   W 1.1 cm   DIAM. (max.) hoop
2 cm
03226 IS

The emerald is engraved with a quotation from the *Gulestan,* or Rose Garden, of the Persian poet Sa'di: *bolbolā mozhde-ye bahār biyār* (which continues *khabār-e bad be-bum bāz gozar).* 'O Nightingale bring us the tidings of Spring (Return the bad news to the owl)'; Dr Kh. Khatib Rahbar (ed.), *Gulestan,* Tehran, n.d., 1357s /1978 ?, ch. 8, 25, p. 534.

Dr A.S. Melikian-Chirvani, who very kindly translated this, comments that the seal is obviously linked with the Iranian *nowruz* or New Year, which takes place on the first day of spring. It may therefore have been a seal used for marking a *nowruz* gift, or have been a gift made to mark an important event (such as a birth) which took place at *nowruz*.

The stone, which is step-cut at the back and probably Colombian, is in a rather incongruous setting: enclosing the open rectangular bezel are two applied cobras, their bodies encircling the hoop.

96
Ring
Enamelled gold set with an emerald
North India (Varanasi?); c. 1850
H 2.8 cm   w hoop 2 cm
03227 IS

The emerald, set into an octagonal bezel, is probably Colombian and is polished but retains its natural, uneven surface and is foiled. The enamel is translucent green and opaque rose-pink painted over white. According to Rai Krishnadasa (1971, p. 330) pink enamelling was introduced to India from Kabul by a craftsman called Kaiser Agha. He worked for Asaf ad-Daula, Nawab of Oudh, from 1775-97, whose capital was at Lucknow. He had learnt pink enamelling from Iran and the palette became popular in Lucknow; then, 'as Banaras was the atelier of the Lucknow Nawabs, the art was established here soon after. From that time it has become a speciality of Banaras and though it was practised in Delhi and Lucknow also, the artists and their disciples were all from Banaras' *(loc. cit.).* The craft came to an end with the death of its last hereditary master, Babbu Singh, in about 1923. Lotus and rose motifs were usual, and a poetic touch was added by the grinding of the pink enamel in

rose *itr,* or essence of roses. Pink enamel was also used in Sind under the Talpur rulers, again introduced from Iran. This ring was acquired by the Indian Museum in 1855 from an exhibition, and was described as being from Bengal, though Bengal Presidency at this time would have included both Benares (Varanasi) and Delhi.

97
Ring
Enamelled gold set with a ruby
Mughal India; late 18th century?
H 3 cm
BM: 2396

98
Ring
Engraved gold set with a sapphire
Bengal; c. 1850
H 3 cm   W hoop 2.2 cm
03228 IS

The oval sapphire has been cut to produce as large a stone as possible rather than to maximise the colour; there is a marked colour bar across the middle. This characteristic feature of Indian jewellery, where size is the paramount consideration, was noted by Mrs Meer Hassan ᶜAli (1832, p.59). The influence of contemporary Europe is seen in the claw setting of the stone, which is never found in traditional Indian jewellery.

99
Ring
Gold, engraved and set with an engraved sapphire parrot with ruby eyes and almandine garnet beak
Bengal; c. 1850
H 3.1 cm   W (max.) hoop 1.9 cm
03229 IS

This ring was an exhibition piece, acquired in 1855. The maker must at some time have seen drawings, or even actual examples, of European rings where two hands clasp each other indicating love or friendship. That he did not have a model in front of him when he made this is indicated by the fact that the two hands are here resolutely cast asunder to face in opposite directions.

100
Ring
Cast gold bezel, engraved and with applied gold spheres; hoop sheet gold over a lac(?) core
South India; 18th century
H 3.5 cm   DIAM. hoop 2.3 cm; bezel 2.5 cm
IS 28-1980

This finely worked ring has no known parallels and its dating so far is a matter for speculation. Nandi, the bull sacred to Shiva, is seated on a pedestal with the *lingam,* or phallic symbol of Shiva, before him. Enclosing this central image is an inscriptional band in Kannada which has not yet been deciphered. Dr John Marr has pointed out that the thickening of the strokes of the letters is a feature not found in this script before the early 18th century, the result of stylistic influence from the missionary tracts which began to be published then.

Underneath the bezel is a lotus chalice rising out of a band of small spheres which are applied round the shoulders, in a double band with a third band soldered on top. The bevelled hoop is probably filled with lac; the outer edges have been crimped over a strip at the back which covers the solid core. It is engraved with a single line, following the inner contour, and with a lozenge at the base.

Rings · 97

101
Nandi ring
Gold set with rubies, a spinel and a baroque pearl with a diamond 'eye'
South India; 18th century(?)
DIAM. 3.5 cm
BM: 2395
From the Franks Bequest, formerly in the Braybrooke collection

The form of the pearl suggests that of a bull, which is here intended to be Nandi, the animal associated with the god Shiva which is found often at the entrance to Shaivite temples. The flat square support for the pearl and the geometrical arrangement of the eleven rubies and one spinel around it are characteristically southern Indian features (see p. 40).

PUBLISHED
Dalton, 1912, p. 332.

102
Nandi ring
Gold set with a carved sapphire bull
South India; 18th century(?)
DIAM. 2.3 cm
BM: 2394
From the Franks Bequest

PUBLISHED
Dalton, 1912, p. 332.

101 102

103
Ring
Gold set with rubies and sapphires, the jewelled sections applied on to the sheet gold hoop
South India; 19th century
DIAM. 4 cm
BM: 2401

103

This ring came from the collection of Alessandro Castellani, acquired by the British Museum in 1872.

PUBLISHED
Dalton, 1912, p. 333.

104
Mirror ring *(arsi)*
Gold set with rubies and green beryls, the back with a stamped floral scroll
Northern India (Panjab?); 19th century
DIAM. 4 cm
Lent by the Trustees of the Ashmolean Museum, Oxford: x 2097.

Maclagan, 1890, described in detail the manufacture of rings like these, their backs stamped on dies. He noted that this ornament can be finished in two days (p. 21).

104

I am greatly indebted to Dr F. Brian Atkins, Curator of the Mineral Collections, University Museum, Oxford, for his identification of the stones in this ring.

Anklets

105
Anklet
Engraved gold rosettes, set alternately with diamonds or lidded and set with precious or semi-precious stones
Calcutta; c. 1850
DIAM. 10.2 cm
03182 IS

This was acquired from exhibition as an anklet; despite the usual restrictions on wearing gold on the feet the diameter would be too great for a conventional armlet. Each alternate rosette is lidded and foiled in a colour which matches its stone. The stones, beginning with the pearl and moving clockwise, are: blue sapphire, ruby, diamond, emerald, yellow sapphire, spinel, chrysoberyl cat's eye, hessonite garnet, turquoise and coral.

PUBLISHED
Hendley, vol. XII, fig. 756.

106
Pair of anklets
Gold with applied lozenges and stamped spheres imitating granulation
L 10.8 cm W 8 cm
Madras; c. 1850
03481 IS

The imitation granulation was done by stamping sheet gold onto a shaped depression in a jeweller's mould (cf. no. 125).

Anklets · 99

107 (one only illustrated)
Pair of anklets
Cast silver, chased and with an engraved inscription
Baroda (Dabhoi); late 19th century
H 10.5 cm DIAM. 14 cm (max.)
IM 286-1927

For religious reasons, gold ornaments were not usually worn on the feet (see p. 120). These dramatic silver anklets, inscribed as having been made at Dabhoi, demonstrate clearly that this did not mean foot jewellery was therefore lacking in value or ostentation.

Jewellery made for Europeans

108
Seal ring of Sir John Shore (1751-1834)
Gold set with an engraved emerald; the seal Indian, dated 1797 in Arabic numerals; the gold ring added by Townshend
Seal W 2.1 cm H 1.7 cm
1283-1869
From the Townshend collection

This ring came from the collection of precious stones bequeathed to the museum by the Rev. Chauncy Hare Townshend (1798-1868) and originally belonged to H.P. Hope (d. 1839) whose famous collection included the Hope diamond. All the stones were mounted as rings which were predominantly in standardised settings such as the coronet type seen here.

The seal is inscribed in Persian 'Sir John Shore Baronet Bahadur'. Sir John Shore began his Indian career as a writer in the East India Company's Civil Service (in 1769, in Calcutta) and ended it as Governor-General from 1793 to 1798.

In the eighteenth century the enormously wealthy leading British figures in India consciously adopted the habits of the Nawabs, or provincial rulers (see p. 43). Though fob seals would have been more usual in contemporary Britain and were certainly made for Company servants, Sir John Shore followed indigenous fashions by having a seal ring. India followed the age-old Near Eastern tradition of using seals rather than signatures to mark documents. Emerald seals seem to have been particularly treasured in the eighteenth century; in 1723 the emperor Muhammad Shah had presented the head of a famous banking family with 'a fine emerald seal with his title of Jagat Seth engraved upon it desiring he would preserve it and hand it down to his posterity' (J. H. Little, 'The House of Jagatseth' part 1, *Bengal Past & Present*, vol. 20, Calcutta 1920, p. 149). The inscription is in Persian as this was the *lingua franca* of India throughout the Mughal period.

PUBLISHED
B. Hertz, *Catalogue of the Collection of Pearls and Precious Stones formed by H. P. Hope*, 1839, p. 45, no. 7.
A.H. Church, *Precious Stones Considered in Their Scientific and Artistic Relations. With a Catalogue of the Townshend Collection of Gems in the South Kensington Museum*, London, 1883, p. 106.
Bury, 1982, p. 168, no. 11.

109
Crucifix
Enamelled gold set with diamonds
Northern India; probably mid-18th century
H 6.2 cm W 4.9 cm D 0.6 cm
Lent by Christopher R. Cavey

The earliest references to crucifixes being made by Mughal craftsmen are to be found in the letters of the Jesuits, who came to India with no less an intention than converting the Emperor. In 1595, Jerome Xavier records that Prince Salim (later the emperor Jahangir) visited the Jesuit chapel at Lahore and, having seen a crucifix there, immediately wished to have one 'made in ivory by his own workmen' (C. H. Payne (trs.), *Akbar and the Jesuits*, London, 1926, p. 67). In 1603, Xavier claims to have seen a crucifix carved on an emerald 'about the size of one's thumb', which had been made at Agra, again for the Prince, and was 'encircled with gold, [and] pierced with a holder by which it can be hung on a gold chain'.

This crucifix seems to be an eighteenth-century piece: the sides are enamelled with red poppies on a plain gold ground which compare with motifs on the Watson turban aigrette of c. 1750 (no. 37).

By this time Christianity was well established as one of the many religions to be found in the subcontinent, less the result of the efforts of the proselytizing Jesuits of the sixteenth century than the arrival of European trading companies.

Jewellery made for Europeans · 101

110
Necklace
Enamelled gold, set with pearls and with a plaited gold chain; made by Robert Phillips of 12 Cockspur Street, London, for the Paris Exposition Universelle of 1867 (maker's mark RP in Roman capitals
L 38 cm pendants W 0.9 cm H 2 cm;
549-1868

Mrs Haweis, in her book *The Art of Beauty* (London, 1878, p. 104), described a visit to the Cockspur Street premises: 'Under the direction of Messrs. Phillips, the most perfect models are sought for the ornaments they furnish. Museums and picture galleries are ransacked for devices of necklaces, earrings and pendants.' The perfect model for this piece was an eighteenth-century Mughal thumb ring (no. 94). The motifs and scale of the design of the inner surface of the ring match the pendants exactly; the colour has been copied one side while one of the most characteristic colours found in Indian enamelling, the bright, translucent red, has been used for the other. It is therefore clear that the jeweller must have carefully drawn the design from the ring, which had been in the Indian Museum since 1855, adding an orientalising cusped and lobed frame.

The necklace does not follow Indian techniques of manufacture: each pendant is hollow-cast rather than made in two sections over a lac core. Although the Indian influence could not be more direct, the necklace could never be taken for an Indian piece; when compared with an original the Phillips necklace is neater and almost imperceptibly more mechanical. This is irrelevant to the aesthetic impact; the jeweller has used Indian motifs in his own idiom with brilliant success.

PUBLISHED
Bury, 1982, p. 135, no. 4.

94

110

102 · *Jewellery of the Mughal Period*

111
Ruby ring
Engraved gold, the five Burmese rubies in open claw settings
Madras; c. 1850
H 2.2 cm W hoop 2 cm
03230 IS

Though copied from a slightly earlier European ring type, this was made by an Indian craftsman, probably working in an establishment such as P. Orr & Sons (see no. 122). The non-European features are the slightly irregular spacing of the claws and the engraved flowers on the shoulders which, in their clumsy arrangement and lack of rhythm, show little confidence of handling foreign motifs.

112 113 111

113
Emerald ring
Five table-cut emeralds open-set in a cast gold and pierced hoop and bezel
Madras; c. 1850
H 2.2 cm W 2 cm
03111 IS

The emeralds are set into a grid-like system of bars, held at the outer edges by the tips of the openwork hearts on the shoulders of the bezel, which curve round slightly to form claws. Like no. 112, it is copied from European rings of about 1830, but again there is a slight lack of precision in its manufacture and the grids are deeper than would be expected.

112
Ruby ring
Single open-set ruby in cast gold setting
Madras; c. 1850
H 2.2 cm W 1.9 cm
03122 IS

This is closer to its European source which would probably date from the 1830s, during the revival for rococo swirling motifs. However, when compared with western examples, it is slightly heavier and less precisely made.

114
Necklace
Engraved gold set with rubies, diamonds and pastes
Madras; c. 1850
Pendant H 3.8 cm W 4.4 cm
03314 IS

The sliding chain holds a pendant which may also be worn as a brooch. The necklace shows obvious European influence in its form and claw-set stones, but the motifs are larger than its western, continental parallels and the gauge of the metal is slightly thicker. This was acquired by the Indian Museum in 1855 from an exhibition, and was approvingly described as having a 'very chaste design'.

114

115
Brooch
Gold set with six amethysts and one purple glass stone in open settings
Madras; c. 1850
W 3.2 cm
08636 IS

116
Brooch
Gold set with a moonstone and amethysts in open settings, the pin missing
Madras; c. 1850
H 2.5 cm W 3 cm
08637 IS

The moonstone on this brooch is not a perfect oval and would therefore probably have been rejected by a European goldsmith. The claw setting is also rather inferior by contemporary western standards which would have demanded mechanical precision.

117
Pendant
Gold with an amethyst and red and green pastes, open-set
Madras; c. 1850
H 3 cm W 2.8 cm
08639 IS

This was originally a brooch but the pin is now missing.

118
Dragonfly brooch
Gold and gold filigree set with rubies and turquoise on the wings and pastes on the body
Madras; c. 1850
H 4.9 cm W 7.2 cm
08661 IS

Though European in inspiration, this could not be mistaken for a western brooch. Its large size, and the clusters of granules, arranged in groups of three around the edges of the wings, betray its Indian origins. The *cannetille* technique (see Glossary), which enjoyed considerable popularity in the early decades of the century in the west, was by 1850 rather outmoded.

PUBLISHED
Hendley, vol. XII, fig. 644.

118
115 116
117

Jewellery made for Europeans · 105

119
Necklace
Chased gold over coloured glass, set in gold
Indore; c. 1850
L 41 cm
03083 IS

The plaques show the *avatars,* or incarnations of Vishnu, with pride of place being given to Krishna, the eighth incarnation and the deity who has a great many devotees in this part of India.

In the nineteenth century, the towns of Indore and Rutlam in Madhya Pradesh and Partabgarh in southern Rajasthan achieved widespread fame for their characteristic jewellery. The goldsmiths there made ornaments of plaques of glass, gold and silver, the glass being poured into gold or silver frames with a delicate tracery of fine gold pressed onto the glass before it hardened. The motifs cut into the gold were taken equally from Hindu mythology or from Mughal courtly hunting scenes. The glass was either blue (see also no. 120), green or red (no. 121). The plaques were popular locally, having a variety of uses (see no. 124 for plaques set into a miniature temple) but were also exported (see p. 44). The forms of much of the jewellery surviving today are European, suggesting a large western market.

106 · *Jewellery of the Mughal Period*

120
Brooch
Chased gold over blue glass, set in gilt silver
Partabgarh, Indore or Rutlam
H 5.8 cm W 5.8 cm
03078 IS

Jewellery made for Europeans · 107

121
Brooch
Chased gold over red glass, set in gold
Rutlam; c. 1875
W 5.5 cm
Lent by Gracious Permission of Her Majesty
the Queen

This brooch, with a necklace and crucifix, was presented to the Prince of Wales during his tour of India by the Raja of Rutlam, in 1876. The brooch is inscribed 'HRH Prince of Wales Her RH Princess of Wales Rutlam 1876', the inscription encircling what are intended to be portraits of the royal couple. The craftsman has, however, copied the eighteenth-century chintz designs of Europeans seated behind a table which bears bottles and cups. A contemporary touch is given by the inclusion of a candelabra above the couple.

PUBLISHED
Catalogue of the Marlborough House Collection, p. 14, no. 215.

122
Swami **work bracelet**
Gold, worked in repoussé on a ring-matted ground, inscribed P. Orr and Sons
Madras; c. 1875
L 19 cm H 2.9 cm
Lent by Mrs Sheila Horsbrugh

This flexible bracelet composed of six hollow plaques was one of the most popular items made by P. Orr and Sons. It echoes, in its heaviness of design, the 'archaeological' jewellery of contemporary Europe, pioneered by the Castellani firm and also made by craftsmen such as Carlo Giuliano and John Brogden (see Gere, 1972, p. 102 ff.).

The style, known as *swami* work, is described in the firm's advertising brochure issued after the Prince of Wales' tour of India of 1875-76; '*Swami work* is peculiar to Southern India, and represents in *alto-relievo* or embossed style, distinct designs or figures of Heathen deities or "Swamies" of the Hindu Pantheon'. The firm had presented several items to the Prince, and claimed an international market for its wares. The brochure states that all gold jewellery was worked in Sovereign (i.e. 22 carat) gold and then stamped ORR 22 (on this piece, the stamp is on the clasp). The work was apparently done by local craftsmen 'under European superintendence'. The deities, all identified by inscriptions giving their south Indian names, include Vishnu (and his fish incarnation), Shiva, Ganesha and Sarasvati.

Miscellany

123
Pair of shoes
Chased sheet silver and gold over wood
Kutch; second half of the 19th century
H 13 cm L 27 cm
Private collection

These shoes were probably intended for use in the shrine of a deity; as they symbolise the deity, the usual prohibition against wearing gold on the feet would not apply.

124
Portable shrine
Silver, cast, chased and partly worked in repousse on a ring-matted ground with insets of glass and gold; enamelled details; the partly-gilt figures with ruby eyes; inscriptional plaque at the back inlaid with niello
Rajasthan; dated 1879 vs/1822 AD
H 31 cm W 17.25 cm
Private collection

This portable shrine, according to the inscription, was made 'on the 13th day of the dark half of the month of Karttika, 1879 *samvat*' [for, or in the name of] Sir John Malik'. Dr Rupert Snell, who very kindly read and translated the inscription, adds that the weight of the temple is given as 96 tolas of silver.

'Sir John Malik', as suggested by Robert Skelton, must be intended for Sir John Malcolm, who administered Central India (which included the centres which produced this kind or work – see nos. 119-21) from 1818 until the end of 1821. The date on the temple converts to October or November 1822, which means it must have been commissioned before he left India and, in time-honoured fashion, was not completed by the goldsmith for the required date. During his administration, Malcolm wrote his detailed *Memoir of Central India,* which covers the economic condition of the area, with much information on the different castes and tribes living there. Unfortunately, the goldsmiths are completely glossed over.

The shrine is in the form of a temple with three niches on a pedestal base containing the images of Rama (with a bow), Vishnu and Lakshmi at the centre, and the monkey god Hanuman. Above the niches are the elephant god Ganesha and Shiva in applied repoussé panels. The glass and gold insets depict various Hindu deities including the *avatars*, or incarnations of Vishnu; Shiva (as an ascetic, the pierced plaques backed with red fabric); Garuda, the half-man, half-bird *vahana* or mount of Vishnu (top left), and again, Ganesha, the remover of obstacles and one of the most popular deities in Hindu mythology.

124▶

125
Jeweller's mould
Cast brass, deeply incised
India; 20th century?
DIAM. 14.5 cm
Lent by Christopher R. Cavey

When a goldsmith needs to produce endless, identical repetitions of small motifs, he may use a mould, hammering sheet gold or silver into a preformed depression on the metal block. Jewellers' moulds usually have a utilitarian appearance in keeping with their function; this example, with its golden colour and pleasing arrangement of small motifs, is probably at least as attractive as the jewellery it produced.

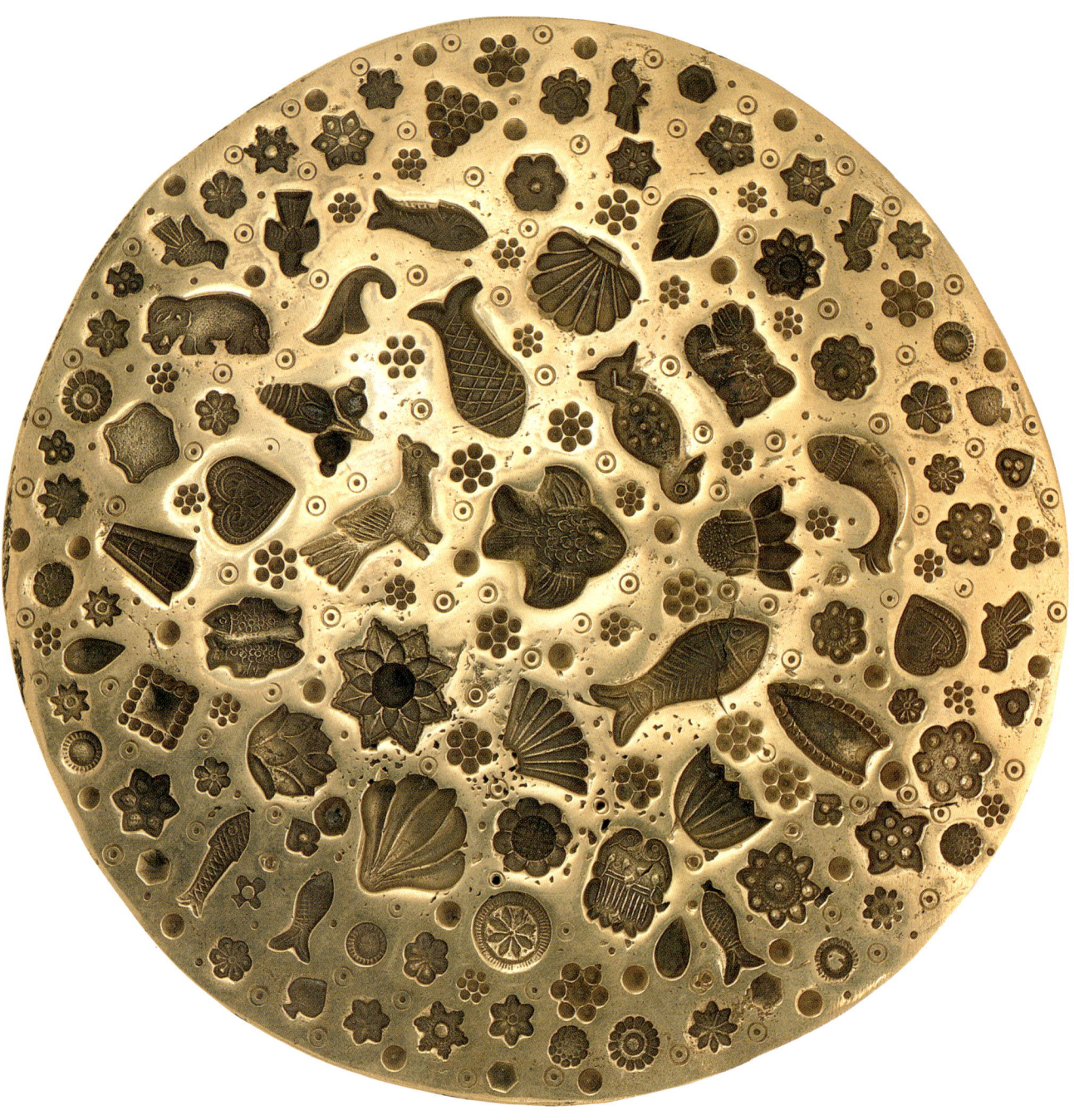

Naga Jewellery

126
Necklace of *buprestid* beetle cases
Worn by a young man; Benroumi village,
Zemi Naga, Assam
L 52.5 cm
Pitt Rivers Museum: 1934.82.17

PUBLISHED
Insects in Art exhibition held at the Ashmolean
Museum, Oxford, 10 March–16 April, 1987.

112 · *Jewellery of the Mughal Period*

127
Necklet
Cast brass with applied, cast pendants
Naga Hills; worn by Konyak men and women
H (max.) 15 cm W (max.) 20.3 cm
Pitt Rivers Museum: 1945.10.94

This necklet was collected on 27 October 1922 by Professor Henry Balfour on his tour of the Naga Hills, according to his diary. He notes later that it was 'made to the E., somewhere towards, or in, the Singpho country', and that it cost 5 rupees. A similar necklet, described as the insignia of a head-hunter, was exhibited in Geneva in 1982 (Barbier, 1982, pl. 6).

128
Man's armlet
Coiled brass with trumpet-shaped terminals with dotted decoration
Naga Hills (Kacha Naga, South Barail Range)
H 12 cm DIAM. 9.4–9.6 cm
Pitt Rivers Museum

This armlet, one of a pair, would have been worn on the upper arm; the 1902 photograph of the Kabrii boy shows him wearing a similar example (fig. 20). A comparable pair are in the Barbier-Muller Museum, Geneva (Barbier, 1982, pl. 28).

129
Three cast brass bangles

Top: Kacha Nagas, South Barail Range, Naga Hills
H 11 cm
Pitt Rivers Museum; VII. 72
Presented by Col. L.W. Shakespear in 1923

This bangle, according to its donor, was worn with the points at the back. It has lightly incised chevron decoration towards the points.

Below left: East Angami, Naga Hills
H 9 cm W terminals 3 cm
Pitt Rivers Museum: dd. J.H. Hutton, 1931

This was worn by women. It is decorated at the terminals with incised circles arranged in lozenges.

Below right: Tengima Angami, Naga Hills
H 8 cm W 5.6 cm
Pitt Rivers Museum: dd J.H. Hutton 1931

This, again, is a woman's bangle and has chevron motifs on the recurving points.

The Darker Side of Gold

Gold has always exercised a mysterious influence on the human mind throughout the world. A metal whose main functional use[1] is ornamentation depends on the peculiarities of human psychology for its continuing power. If, through some unlikely process, gold should be demystified and no longer perceived as valuable, it would have a catastrophic effect on world markets. Obviously this is not going to happen, but why does gold have such an appeal?

Perhaps the most appropriate country to examine for the motivating forces behind the acquisition of gold is India, which reportedly has the largest holding of gold in private hands, estimated at around 7,000 tonnes. The Reserve Bank of India has nearly 3,000 tonnes. The often quoted complaint of Pliny the Elder (c. AD 23–79) against India sucking in all the gold from Rome in exchange for its textiles and spices reveals an obsession with the metal that has persisted to the present day.

The use of gold in India involves a huge cross-section of goldsmiths[2], retailers, dealers, middle-men and pawn-brokers on the one hand and an eager consumer public on the other. The latter are also substantial suppliers of the raw material, for of the 150 tonnes of gold bought in 1986–7, 50 tonnes was recycled from old ornaments, 2 to 3 tonnes came from the Kolar and Hutti gold fields of Karnataka in south India, and the remainder was smuggled into the country in the form of biscuits or ingots (usually through the Middle East) from South Africa. Ironically, India has an embargo on trade with South Africa.

The Gold Control Act[3] of 1963 restricted trade and imports but has not managed to control either the smuggling or the almost atavistic desire that many Indians seem to have for gold. This desire is partly based on a shrewd sense of business. Gold can be depended upon to appreciate steadily in value, particularly in India, where prices are the highest in the world. In November 1987, they rose to an unprecedented Rs.3,744 for 10 grammes, against an international price of Rs.1,700.[4] Inflation and a weak rupee have made gold a popular form of investment and 13 per cent of the country's savings is in gold and silver, either in the form of ornaments or as bulk metal. Spiralling prices do not seem to have checked the nation's preoccupation with buying gold, and since the prices are not fixed by the Government but are subject to the vagaries of market forces this encourages speculation and manipulation and provides a fertile breeding ground for smugglers.

The price of gold can be a conversation starter on trains and buses, with people marvelling at the new heights it has reached, reminiscing about a time when it was cheap and bemoaning the fact that the soaring cost made it difficult for them to buy gold for daughters' weddings. The custom of giving gold (along with gifts in cash and kind) as dowry when a daughter is getting married is regarded as one of the most important contributing factors towards the Indians' compulsion to buy gold. Generally a middle-class family will give 10–15 tolas of gold (a tola is

Fig. 22
Two Bharatnatyam dancers:
Indira Thiagarajah and
Chitralekha Bolar.
1987
Studio Colophon, Leicester

11.6 grammes) to a daughter when she gets married. Among the business communities – the Banias, for instance, who are merchants from the Marwari caste – as much as 100 tolas can be given. The giving of gold is not necessarily a straightforward economic transaction. Frequently it is a way of expressing love and affection, and even families that are poor try to buy some gold for their offspring. Nor is the giving of gold confined only to the family of the bride; the husband's family is also expected to give some items of jewellery to the new daughter-in-law. Gold and femininity are intimately linked. The nature of women's supposed attachment to gold in India can be attributed to the fact that it gives them a measure of economic independence after they are married and an autonomous identity, however partial this may be. Ostensibly gold is given by a girl's family to protect her from possible hardships, such as desertion by the husband or loss of employment within the family. According to Hindu marriage law, when a man is declared bankrupt, all his assets can be seized, but not his wife's gold, brought in as *stridhana* or dowry. But the interpretation of whether a dowry is a gift to the daughter or to the daughter's husband is fraught with complications. What is supposedly extended as financial protection towards the daughter can be a straitjacket, as dowry demands for gold and money escalate between the period of engagement and marriage. There have been several cases where the bridegroom's family refused to proceed with the wedding ceremony until the gold given by the bride's family had been carefully weighed.

The last fifteen years have seen a spate of what the press term 'dowry deaths' or 'bride burnings', which have caused considerable controversy and outrage. Parents-in-law, often aided by only too willing sons, demand money and gold from the daughter-in-law's family, until they have been squeezed dry; then they resort to the simple expedient of eliminating the bride. This appalling practice received fresh notoriety with the suspected suicide of a young wife in Tiptur in Karnataka in November 1987, because of reported dowry demands by her in-laws. The fierce public reaction to this death is an indication of changing attitudes, but as yet this is only a glimmer.

Although anti-dowry legislation appears punitive on paper, gold is inextricably linked with the marriage system, and as a goldsmith in Baroda confidently stated to the author: 'As long as there are marriages in India, there will be ample work for goldsmiths'. This was borne out in Jaipur's bustling Johari Bazaar recently, where a crowd of people had collected outside a jeweller's shop, even before the shutters were up. As soon as it was opened, as many people as could squeeze into the shop rushed in and the shutters were lowered again, leaving a disconsolate throng outside. This, I was assured by a local Jaipur resident, was a daily occurrence throughout the year and not a momentary stampede caused by the marriage season.[5]

Migration does not seem to affect this pattern. Indians abroad buy as avidly as their compatriots in the subcontinent, though a number of them bemoan the fact that their relatively stronger economic position makes them vulnerable to the requests of relatives in India for money to buy gold for family weddings. A few take out second mortgages or capitalise on insurance policies that have not yet matured in order to raise the money.

Fig. 23
Gold beater; 1822
The goldsmith's sacred thread and ash markings on his forehead indicate that he is a Brahmin; usually goldsmiths come from the Vaishya caste.
BBC Hulton Picture Library

Predictably, wherever there is a substantial Indian community abroad, goldsmiths' shops are established, for instance, in Britain, America, Hong Kong, Singapore and Malaysia. Most of these are retail outlets, selling gold crafted in India. In Britain the commonly-used 9 carat gold is thought by Indians to be wholly unsuitable for their jewellery, which has to be 22 carat to pass muster.

Normally, Indian goldsmiths both at home and abroad are following a hereditary trade and come from the Vaishya caste. However, there is enough flexibility within the system to allow people from different ends of the caste spectrum such as Brahmins (priests) and Mochis (cobblers) to practise as goldsmiths as well (see fig. 23). Traditionally a secretive community and not easily accessible for detailed interviews about their work, most of the goldsmiths I spoke to did not want to be named or even quoted.

For a craft that entails great precision of weight and caratage, a goldsmith's method of gauging the latter seems to be subjective, to say the least. The touchstone, a ubiquitous component of a goldsmith's equipment (along with a pair of scales) is used to judge caratage, according to the colour of the smear left by a piece of gold when rubbed gently on it. In addition, gold's reaction to *shora*,[6] the acid used to purify it, is another gauge of caratage. But ultimately goldsmiths depend on experience coupled with instinct rather than any scientific system.

Understandably, considering the strictures of societal expectation and a galloping gold price, goldsmiths are popularly viewed with suspicion. But when one takes into account the lack of effective official control, one hears relatively few complaints about customers being cheated over the quality of the gold. Weight, however, is another matter, and customers are constantly on their guard to avoid being duped. Goldsmiths seem to share this obsession and in their turn display a grim determination to save every tiny grain of gold that may have been unwittingly lost in the process of beating and cold hammering. At dusk, in the little goldsmiths' gullies[7] of Mysore, small boys sweep the pavements along the shops with a soft brush in an effort to retrieve any particle of gold that may have flown outside. This fanatical care to salvage every speck of the precious metal has created an interesting sub-industry, where regular traders pay goldsmiths a fee for allowing them to collect the dust that accumulates on the floor and furniture of a goldsmith's workplace, which they then process, so that nothing is lost.

Most goldsmiths learn the trade by being apprenticed to practising goldsmiths when they are twelve or thirteen years old. Formal training is virtually unknown, and though the Jamsetjee Jeejeebhoy School of Art in Bombay used to run courses in goldsmithing forty years ago, the rising cost of the metal forced them to close it down. There is an informal training centre in Rajkot in Saurashtra, but this facility is only for members of the goldsmith community. Interestingly enough, Tribhovandas Bhimji Zaveri, a prominent jewellery concern in India, is setting up a training college in goldsmithing in the autumn of 1988, in Karol Bagh in Delhi. The courses will be open to anyone, regardless of caste, who shows an interest in and aptitude for crafting gold.

Primarily a male-dominated occupation, women goldsmiths are rare, but in places like Bijapur and Gulbarga in Karnataka, for example, female members of a goldsmith's family frequently help their male relatives in their work. They never, however, set up separate establishments of their own.

Goldsmiths face health hazards such as damaged lungs caused by frequent blowing into the *bhagna* (a pipe with a bent head, used to melt gold) and impaired eyesight, but a goldsmith working on his own or with one or two apprentices (usually a son or male relative) never refuses commissions. The deadlines are, however, often impossible to meet. The goldsmith may quote a waiting period ranging from a fortnight to three months, but it is not unusual for irate customers to have waited for anything up to two years for a single item of jewellery. Goldsmiths have their own ideas of how to assess priorities, and usually marriage jewellery is considered more important than other pieces; if the wedding is imminent, other orders are calmly shelved.

This perhaps accounts for the phenomenal success of stores like Tribhovandas Bhimji Zaveri in Delhi and Bombay (they are the only jewellers with something of a national reputation in India), with their professionalism and ability to produce quantities of retail jewellery, though the prices are slightly above average. They (and some other major jewellers) hallmark their gold and record the weight on each item. They claim to be the first jewellers to have started doing this, quite voluntarily, from 1965 onwards. Founded in 1857 in Bombay, there are today a number of Zaveri stores, set up by various members of the family.

Although Nand-Kishore Zaveri claims that their customers come from as far away as Bangalore and Madras in the south to buy their gold, paradoxically none of his family are in the habit of wearing gold. The Zaveris have a network of goldsmiths all over the country who supply them with jewellery from every part of India, ranging from the minute gold *thāli* [8] favoured by the Syrian Christian brides of Kerala to the elaborate filigree necklaces of Lucknow and Kanpur. In addition to having a vast display of ready-made pieces, they also take orders for customised jewellery, as do the smaller jewellers who often have no ready-made stock to sell. The Zaveris refuse orders for jewellery under 22 carat gold but make an exception for the gold used in setting diamonds, where 18 carat and sometimes even 14 carat is used, in order to create precise and delicate patterns.[9]

They pride themselves on bringing about a change in recent tastes in diamond jewellery in India. In the past, diamonds were often clumsily set, with large badly-cut stones, though they could have a certain charm of their own. Influenced by western methods of cutting and style, the Zaveris gradually introduced new, more intricate patterns. They also maintain that they do not merely reflect popular taste in the kind of gold jewellery they produce but try to shape and change it by introducing new designs, often apparently western-influenced. There is no real movement within India to create its own distinct contemporary styles in modern jewellery. A new trend means either a revived interest in some of the older forms of Indian jewellery like *kundan*[10] or *mina*-work[11] or western-influenced innovations. But the Zaveris, in spite of their efforts to direct taste, acknowledge that the public remains stubbornly traditional in the gold jewellery it buys. Even the 'élite' groups, who take pleasure in being different, will always have a requisite number of these traditional pieces in their collections.

This is particularly true of marriage jewellery. For instance, the *mangal-sutra*[12] and *thāli*, prevalent in western and southern India, and the elephant bracelets of Bengal are all symbols of marriage and seem to be timeless in their style. In spite of this traditionalism, Indians have very little sentimental attachment to their gold as family heirlooms. These are frequently melted down to produce more 'contemporary' pieces. Surprisingly, a number of goldsmiths and retailers claim that they do not try to capitalise on gold jewellery if it is antique but treat it just as they would any other gold: they pay its scrap value and melt it down.

In a society where gold is valued as much for its weight as for its aesthetic worth, one might have expected craftsmanship to suffer, but this has not invariably been the case. A number of craftsmen in the south produce *mangal-sutras* where the chain is as fine as a hair, with the tiniest of black beads strung on it, and weighing as little as 2 grammes (see no. 169). Considering the fact that the gold used in India is usually 22 carat and therefore extremely soft, such dexterity is even more remarkable. Weight and solidity in a piece of gold jewellery is always of great importance to the buyer. A prominent jeweller remembers the heaviest piece of jewellery ordered as weighing 5 kilograms. Made for a Saudi Arabian princess, it was a full-length dress of gold filigree with a matching yashmak. It took ten goldsmiths, working a twelve-hour shift, four months to complete this unique ensemble.

The Gold Control Act of 1963 has made it illegal for any individual to own more than two kilograms of gold. A friend gleefully told me how her wealthy aunt, when she realised that her house was being raided by the police in 1972, decked out members of her considerable domestic staff with her excess gold and locked the gates of the grounds in case any of them felt inclined to abscond. The ingenuity to acquire and maintain gold seems inexhaustible.

Regardless of the buying price, gold is sold exactly according to the rate in the stock market on any given day. The larger goldsmiths display the price in their shops, but smaller outlets can be more arbitrary. The estimated cost of a piece of gold jewellery when ordered may not coincide with the actual price when it is ready, a point of frustration for customers trying to buy things on a tight budget.

Visits to some of the larger goldsmiths are treated with solemnity not untinged with excitement. Some stores are an amazing spectacle of fitted carpets, acres of plate glass, indoor fountains and pristine cases, in which the gold and diamonds are displayed on dark blue velvet, with discreet rows of sales assistants ranged round the room. The effect is exactly that of a plush Hindi film set, in itself a clever marketing ploy, as if one is entering a *masala*[13] version of fairyland.

This is in interesting contrast to the austere setting of the humble goldsmith who sits in his small dim shop, on a spotless white cushion, with a tiny glass-topped cabinet containing little dishes of coloured stones, most of them paste, though a few may be semi-precious It is the quality of the gold the customer is interested in, not the quality of the stones.

The introduction of other forms of savings such as banks and insurance policies does not seem to have affected the desire to own gold. But what about those who are too poor to buy it? I remember the mother of a farm labourer, who had for most of her life been too poor to afford any gold. Her son became a building contractor and was prosperous in a relatively short time. One of his first acts to celebrate his new-found wealth was to indulge his mother's wistful yearning for gold, and though well into her eighties, her neck and withered arms were laden with the gleaming metal.

Typically, Hindu Indians have managed to rationalise their reverence for gold by giving it a spurious sanctity through quasi-religious connotations. Lakshmi, the goddess of wealth and one of the most popular in the Hindu pantheon, is supposed to dwell in gold. This accounts for the taboo among a large number of Hindus about wearing gold below the hip, since having one's legs or feet touch Lakshmi is disrespectful. Exceptions to this are those of royal birth and the Ursu community of Karnataka who wear anklets and toe-rings of gold.

Sanctifying gold gives people the license to yearn for it, for it is after all sacred. It has even found a place in the body of devotional hymns to Venkateshwara, the popular deity of the Tirupathi temple, where songs are composed in description and praise of the jewellery adorning the image. Indeed, the splendour of the jewellery is treated almost as an organic extension of the deity's physical attributes. For instance the *Saundaryalahari* or *Flood of Beauty*, in the hymn to Parvati, after describing the melodious tinkling of her ear ornaments, goes on to describe the nose stud, which 'holds pearls created by your cool breath.'[14]

In addition to being a symbol of wealth and power, to a society that has traditionally been obsessed with ritual purity, gold is also regarded as 'clean' or 'pure' because of its untarnishability, even after hundreds of years of use. Every important Hindu ritual involves the use of gold by those who can afford it, and some-

The Darker Side of Gold · 121

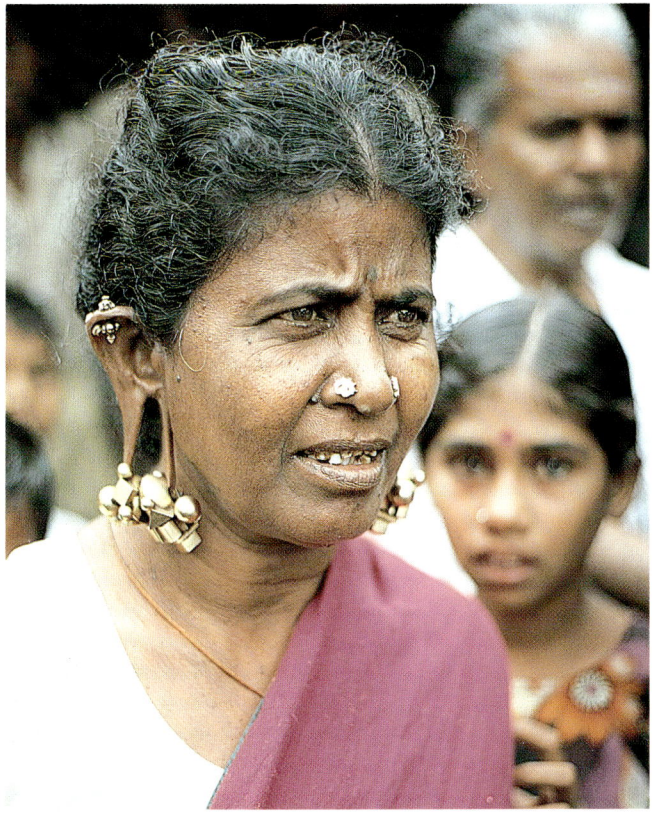

Fig. 24 (left)
A woman from Tamil Nadu
Caroline Washington, Robert Harding Picture Library

Fig. 25 (right)
Bangle-buying at Pushkar camel fair, Rajasthan
Sybil Sassoon, Robert Harding Picture Library

times even by those who cannot. Naming ceremonies, marriages, *graha pravesh* or housewarmings and even deaths, use gold in some form or another. Quite often a tiny nugget of gold is buried when the foundations are being laid for a house, since this is considered auspicious. Unlike precious stones (particularly the diamond which is viewed as possessing a potential for disaster) gold, because of the incumbent Lakshmi, is imbued with qualities that are more benign.

Gold and precious stones have long been regarded as having talismanic properties by a wide variety of cultures. There is a popular belief in India that gold is good for one's physical well-being. For example, cylindrical gold phylacteries are thought to alleviate ailments of the heart and, when children have mumps, the touch of gold against the glands is supposed to help reduce the swelling.

A huge body of mythology has accrued around gold, and man's relationship to this metal has been well documented in oral and recorded folklore, both rural and urban. A curious feature of some of the lore is how it has become incorporated into the design of the jewellery. The image of Lakshmi, for example, is popular because of her association with gold (see no. 130). Similarly, serpents, particularly cobras, which are supposed to be the legendary guardians of treasure are a common motif in Indian jewellery (see nos. 130 and 131).

The sublimation of the Hindu passion for gold into something sacred means that the religious vein is never far from the surface. Ten years ago the regional papers of Karnataka carried the story of a Brahmin family in Mangalore who, after fifteen years of comparative poverty and hardship, managed to donate 500 tolas of gold to the Sri Venkateshwara temple in Tirupathi. The eldest brother of this orthodox priest's family had made a vow to donate it after Sri Venkatesh had appeared to him in a dream and demanded 500 tolas of gold as proof of his devotion. This demand had all the weight of a divine command to the devout but hapless priest. He confided his dilemma to his two younger brothers, who regarded the dream injunction as seriously as he did. For the next fifteen years, they pooled their meagre resources, treating the whole process like a military campaign. They cut down their expenses to the bare minimum and painstakingly started to accumulate the gold until they had the desired quantity which they then, triumphantly and ceremonially, handed to the trustees of that already well endowed temple.

In the corpus of stories concerning gold, cautionary tales also abound – a culture's method of maintaining its own checks and balances over propensities it sees as potentially destructive. Rabindranath Tagore perhaps understood this better than most. In two memorable short stories, 'The Trust Property' and 'The Stolen Jewels', he uses themes that explore the dark ambivalences, motivations and subconscious desires that drive man to seek gold, often at the cost of being dehumanised. 'The Trust Property'[15] has a folktale as its basis, for the protagonist, an old miser, believes in the story of the *yak* or *yakshi* acting as guardian of one's treasures, until one appeared in a future incarnation to reclaim it. The miser has only one other desire that matches this lust: his longing to be with his grandson again. His only son had left in disgust at the father's parsimony and taken his own son with him.

Eventually the old man befriends a homeless waif, a little boy with no connections or attachments. He decides that he is the ideal choice to be made into a *yak*, to safeguard his treasure. After a bizarre *puja* in a derelict temple, he seals the boy in with his money and his gold. The translator's footnote reads: 'The incidents described in this story, now happily a thing of the past, were by no means rare in Bengal at one time ... Such criminally superstitious practices were resorted to by miserly persons under the idea that they themselves would reacquire the treasure in a future state of existence. "When you see me in future birth passing this way, you must make over all this treasure to me. Guard it till then and stir not" was the usual promise exacted from the victim before he became a *yak*. Many were the "true" stories we heard in childhood of people becoming suddenly rich by coming across ghostly custodians of wealth belonging to them in a past birth.' The twist to the tale is that the little *yak* is none other than the demented miser's yearned-for grandson.

Tagore's second tale, 'The Lost Jewels'[16] (which was made into a film by Satyajit Ray), examines a more subtle and insidious theme than 'The Trust Property'. Mani is a woman so obsessed by her jewellery that consideration for her besotted husband and his business problems are totally overwhelmed by her fear that he will sell her jewellery to raise cash. The gold is presented as a child-substitute, because Mani is childless. Not only has her obsession caused the loss of all sense of perspective and balance (she trusts her blatantly villainous cousin to effect her escape from a supposedly grasping husband) but she is transformed into a lost, haunted creature, inhabiting the twilight regions of the supernatural, after fleeing by boat with her cousin, wearing all her jewellery in order to safeguard it.

This kind of loss of judgement is always a fall from grace in Tagorean terms, and her mysterious end relegates her into some curious purgatorial limbo, which comes closest to Tagore's vision of retribution.

The attitude to gold in India can be summed up as a strange amalgam of shrewdness and irrationality, flashes of insight coupled with an almost transcendent longing. Largely subterranean in its presence, it underlines a universal human tendency to imbue the symbol with greater importance than the contents, resulting in the curious paradox of a supposedly poor country being the largest private repository of this metal on earth.

Footnotes

1. Gold of course has a small range of practical uses. For instance, since the advent of micro-processors gold, because of its high conductivity, is used on connector points.

2. The terms 'goldsmith' and 'jeweller' are used interchangeably in this essay, reflecting the way they are used in India.

3. This act was introduced by the then Finance Minister, Morarji Desai, who, interestingly enough, in 1978, as Prime Minister, relaxed the Control sufficiently to allow gold auctions to take place. The aim of the Act was to regulate the use of gold and indirectly, through that, lessen the Indian attraction for the metal. Initially the Act imposed a ban on any jewellery that was of more than 14 carat gold. This, however, created widespread public protest and had to be quickly withdrawn. The Act also stipulates that all gold bought by jewellers and goldsmiths should be registered; but since demand far outweighs official supplies, this is not always adhered to.

4. Several reasons are proposed for this astronomical rise, the main ones being the steady decline in share prices in India, indirectly affected by the stockmarket crash in the West, and the relatively increased recent success of Customs and Excise in apprehending smuggled gold.

5. Though Hindus on average buy more gold than the Muslims and Christians, the latter have not remained totally unaffected by this preoccupation. Muslims, particularly men, are supposed to eschew gold because of its implications of pomp and splendour, but the women show a marked fondness for gold and silver jewellery. Among the Syrian Christians of Kerala and Mangalore Christians of Karnataka gold forms a necessary part of a girl's dowry.

6. *Shora* is a non-standardized mixture of concentrated acids, including nitric and hydrochloric acids.

7. Gullies: narrow back streets.

8. See Glossary.

9. The higher the caratage the softer the gold is, which makes it correspondingly more difficult to fashion delicate shapes. Twenty-four carat gold is gold at its purest, and only the simplest of jewellery can be fashioned out of this. Strangely enough, some traditional goldsmiths in the south set diamonds only in 24 carat gold, the reasoning being that the king of stones deserves the best of gold.

10. See p. 30.

11. See Glossary.

12. See Glossary.

13. A mixture of spices that forms the basis of some of the curry sauces.

14. *Sandaryalahari* or *Flood of Beauty* is traditionally ascribed to Shankaracharya, an Indian religious reformer who lived in the 8th century and propounded the *advaita* or non-dualistic philosophy. Translated and edited by W. Norman Brown, Harvard University Press, 1958, p.72.

15. *More Stories from Tagore*, London, 1951.

16. *Ibid*.

Twentieth-century Jewellery

130
Necklace with pendant *(kokke-thathi)*
Gold, the repoussé pendant set with graduated cabochon rubies and seed pearls, filled with lac, with chain of 'gund' or hollow gold beads
Coorg, Karnataka, South India; 20th century
Chain: L 60 cm; pendant: H 4.5 cm L 2.5 cm
W 0.3 cm; 39 grammes
Private collection

Though not a symbol of marriage like the *pathak* (no. 131) the *kokke-thathi* belongs to the body of marriage jewellery because it is mandatory for a Coorg bride to wear it. The large crescent-shaped pendant has an image of the seated Lakshmi, goddess of wealth, flanked by two birds that could be peacocks or *garudas*. The pendant is crowned by a cobra with distended hood, which is a multiple symbol of wealth, the male principle and propitiation (an acknowledgement that snakes are a daily hazard of life in richly wooded Coorg). For reasons that are not entirely clear, it was customary for the chain to be a standard length of 26 inches. Perhaps this length was best suited for the magnificence of the pendant to be displayed to advantage. It has become popular to have earrings that match the pendant, without the cobra.

131
Necklace with pendant (pathak)
Gold, half sovereign pendant framed by coral,
surmounted by a cobra with a fresh water
pearl; chain of gold and coral beads and
twisted strands of black glass beads
Coorg, Karnataka, South India; 20th century
Pendant H 2.5 cm L 4.5 cm; chain L 42 cm;
15 grammes
Private collection

The *pathak* is essential for every married
Coorg woman, the black beads and corals
demonstrating her married status (widows
should not wear either). The pendant can
either be an English sovereign or
half-sovereign, or a gold coin with the image
of Lakshmi engraved on it. Like the
kokke-thathi (no. 130) this is also surmounted
by a cobra, backed by a gooseberry shaped
bead, a symbol of fertility, that is not visible
when the *pathak* is worn. The *pathak* is a
variation of the *mangal-sutra,* a necklace of
black beads strung on gold (see no. 169), with
a gold disc-shaped pendant. Commonly worn
in a variety of styles in western and southern
India and, like the *pathak* denoting marriage, it
has now become fashionable for married
women from different regions and cultures,
including the north and the east, to wear a
mangal-sutra.

126 · The Darker Side of Gold

132 133

132
Bracelet (*kadga*)
Gold, the hollow, faceted bangle ornamented with applied twisted wire and set with small rubies
Coorg, Karnataka, South India; 20th century
DIAM. 6 cm H 0.5 cm; 16 grammes
Private collection

The *kadga* is also a piece of marriage jewellery. Comprising two narrow rounded gold bands linked by gold beads, it creates an effect that is both striking and finely wrought. *Kadgas* with triple rather than double bands are also popular.

133
Gold bracelet
Gold with applied cut-work decoration
Kanpur, Uttar Pradesh, North India; 20th century
DIAM. 6 cm H 0.3 cm; 15 grammes
Private collection

This bracelet is typical of the jewellery produced in Lucknow and Kanpur, places which also excel in delicate filigree work. Most of the jewellers are Muslim, and their work has a characteristic stamp, with geometric and linked floral motifs predominating.

134
Gold bracelet with *mina* work
Gold with applied red enamel and open-work decoration
Bombay, Maharashtra, Western India; 20th century
DIAM. 7 cm H 1.4 cm; 35 grammes
Private collection

Mina work, or enamelling, is usually in blue, green, black or red. The rich gold of this surprisingly heavy bracelet is set off by the glowing ruby enamel applied to the linked half-circles of raised gold that decorate the main band, slightly separated from the narrow top and bottom bands. Though the bracelet is close to a traditional Maharashtrian design, it has elements of *art nouveau* about it. The bracelet has minute flexible bells wired to it, which produce a gentle tinkling sound when the bracelet is moved.

Twentieth-century Jewellery · 127

135 136

135
Filigree gold bracelet
Gold, the filigree and cut-work half band fitted onto a bracelet of black plastic
Calcutta, Eastern India; 20th century
DIAM. 7 cm H 0.5 cm; 19 grammes
Private collection

This striking and unusual bracelet of hammered and drawn wire, which is plugged into the plastic band that holds it in place, is a traditional piece of jewellery in Bengal. Originally, the black plastic bangle would have been made of buffalo horn.

136
Elephant bracelet
Gold, on a shellac core with ring-matting
Calcutta, West Bengal, Eastern India; 20th century
DIAM. 6.5 cm H 0.3 cm 20 grammes
Private collection

Commonly referred to as *balaya* or *karā*, this bracelet is a symbol of marriage for Bengali women, in the same manner as the conch-shell bracelet. After the husband's death, these bracelets are no longer worn by the widow. Though the heads at the ends of the bracelets are intended to be elephants, they are so stylised as to resemble *makaras*.

137
Elephant bracelet
Gold, on an iron core, with elephant heads
Calcutta, West Bengal, Eastern India; 20th century
DIAM. 6 cm H 0.1 cm; 11 grammes
Private collection

Bengali wives traditionally wear a plain iron bangle next to the skin in order to avert the evil eye from their husbands and also as an acceptance of the pain of life. But a gold-loving community has managed to embellish even this exceedingly plain ornament by encasing it in gold. As with the elephant bracelet above (no. 136) once the husband dies, the bracelet is no longer worn.

128 · The Darker Side of Gold

138
Necklace (*mohanmāle*)
Ribbed gold beads with moulded decoration
Mysore, South India; 20th century
L 41 cm; 15 grammes
Private collection

Necklaces made up of a variety of hollow gold beads are popular throughout the Indian subcontinent. The beads are frequently patterned on berries and fruit: the *nelli-kai māl*, for instance, is shaped like the gooseberry, and the *mattar māl* like the chickpea.

139
Necklace (*jomāle*)
Gold with grooved moulded beads strung on black cord
Coorg, Karnataka, South India; 20th century
L 71 cm; 20 grammes
Private collection

Along with the *kokke-thathi* (no. 130) and the *pathak* (no. 131) the *jomāle* is considered a necessary part of the Coorg bride's wedding jewellery. The black thread on which the beads are strung makes it particularly auspicious, since the black beads of the *pathak* and the black glass bangles a bride wears on her wedding day are thought to bring luck.

140

Necklace of gold and chalcedony
Gold, the chain set with five chalcedony pendants encased in twisted open-work gold wire
Mysore, Karnataka, South India; 20th century
L 40.5 cm; 34 grammes
Private collection

The pendants, which seem to be stained green chalcedony, are carved in the shape of a leaf. The carving of semi-precious stones like amethysts and aquamarines is popular in India and is frequently done to disguise a flaw in the stone.

141

Chalcedony ring
Gold, the globular chalcedony encased in twisted, open-work gold wire
Mysore, Karnataka, South India; 20th century
DIAM. 1.5 cm H 2 cm; 3 grammes
Private collection

142

Earrings
Gold, the open-work gold wire encasing the globular chalcedony stones
Mysore, Karnataka, South India; 20th century
L 4 cm; 8 grammes
Private collection

130 · *The Darker Side of Gold*

143
Earrings of duck feathers and gold
Gold, the pendant duck feathers topped by small flat decorative tassels of gold, surmounted by studs of white spinel, set in gold
Jammu, Kashmir, North India; 20th century
H 6 cm L 4 cm; 6 grammes
Private collection

The rather unusual use of duck feathers for the earrings is in fact a traditional practice in Jammu and the neighbouring areas in Kashmir. Feathers are more commonly used as adornment by tribal communities. The black feathers of this particular species of duck are supposed to bring good luck.

144
Gold and emerald drops
Gold, the emeralds, imitation pearls, white spinels and diamonds claw set, with springs of gold wire and dangling green and white glass beads
Lahore, Pakistan; 20th century
H 7.5 cm L 2.75 cm; 17 grammes
Private collection

143 144

This pair of earrings typifies much Indian jewellery, where reasonably good stones like the small emeralds and the larger diamonds at the bottom are mixed with white spinels and glass beads.

145
Emerald and pearl earrings
Enamelled gold, with open-set emeralds and pearls
Dhaka, Bangladesh; 20th century
H 0.75 cm W 0.75 cm; 2 grammes
Private collection

In contrast with no. 144, these earrings have been set in a minimal amount of gold. This indicates not only that prices have affected fashions in jewellery but also that tastes have changed, particularly among the middle class. A simple, almost western pattern manages to retain a distinctive touch of the Indian subcontinent, through the subtle use of two tiny horn-shaped protuberances in green enamelled gold.

146
147 145
148 149

146
Saptaratna earrings
Gold, with open-set emeralds, amethysts, sapphires, corals, pearls, spinels and citrines and applied granulation
Dhaka, Bangladesh; 20th century
DIAM. 0.5 cm; 2 grammes
Private collection

The *saptaratna* (seven gems) and *pancharatna* (five gems) are variations on *navaratna* (nine gem) jewellery which has had an enduring popularity throughout the Indian subcontinent. In *navaratna* settings (see no. 83), each gem represents a planet; together they are considered to bring good luck. *Navaratna*, *pancharatna* and *saptaratna* sets seem to be commonly given as part of a bride's dowry.

147
Earrings
Gold, with minute emeralds, rubies and spinels in an open setting
Dhaka, Bangladesh; 20th century
H 10.75 cm L 5 cm; 2 grammes
Private collection

The earrings, with their matching pendant (no. 148), are in the traditional *tikka* or tear-drop shape. Small pieces of jewellery encrusted with tiny stones are popular light jewellery today, and are usually designed as sets.

148
Pendant
Gold, with emeralds, rubies and spinels in an open setting
Dhaka, Bangladesh; 20th century
H 0.2 cm L 0.5 cm; 2 grammes
Private collection

149
Enamelled pendant
Gold, with black enamel
Dhaka, Bangladesh; 20th century
H 1.2 cm L 0.75 cm; 3 grammes
Private collection

Presented by a grandmother to her grandson on his first birthday, the calligraphic inscription in Arabic reads 'Allah'. Muslim men are supposed to eschew jewellery, and this perhaps accounts for the elegant austerity of the piece, where only a minimal amount of gold, proclaiming the name of God, is visible.

150
***Bini* bangle**
Gold, twisted and plaited
Dhaka, Bangladesh; 20th century
DIAM. 6.2 cm; 11 grammes
Private collection

Bangles of this thickness are usually worn in pairs. Bangles are a requisite part of any girl's dowry and are normally given in even numbers, half a dozen or a dozen being the most popular figure. Bangles are almost always made purely of gold in a variety of standard patterns of which this is an example. Diamond-cut bangles, where the gold has been faceted to create maximum sparkle, is extremely popular. Gold bangles of this kind are often worn interspersed with colourful glass bangles.

132 · The Darker Side of Gold

151
Necklace (rānīhār)
Gold, pierced and chased, set with red and white stones
E. Africa; 20th century
Outer chain L 56 cm; middle chain L 34 cm; inner chain L 24.5 cm; 130 grammes
Private collection

Typical of 'investment' jewellery, the necklace is impressive rather than beautiful. Its unusually heavy weight indicates that it was regarded as an asset rather than a piece of ornamentation. This is borne out by the fact that the owner of the piece has not worn it since her wedding day, since she finds its weight irksome.

Nos. 151–67 (except no. 165) are from east Africa, influenced by designs and motifs from the Panjab.

152 *(opposite)*
Bracelet with chain and rings (pancha)
Gold, pierced and chased, set with red and white stones
E. Africa; 20th century
Bracelet DIAM. 6.5 cm H 0.6 cm; length of chain with rings 14 cm; four rings DIAM. 0.5 cm H 2.6 cm; thumb ring DIAM. 0.7 cm H 2.6 cm; 100 grammes
Private collection

This extremely elaborate piece of jewellery called *pancha* meaning five (since there are rings for each finger of the hand) is usually worn by North Indian brides on their wedding day. This piece is also called *ratan-chūṛ*. The disc on the back of the palm, called *hasta padma*, usually represents the sun or the moon. A silver example from Rajasthan may be seen in fig. 25.

Twentieth-century Jewellery · 133

152
153 154 155

153
Hair ornament (pasa)
Gold, chased and pierced, with white and red stones, imitation pearls and red glass beads
E. Africa; 20th century
H 13.5 cm   L 7 cm; 30 grammes
Private collection

The *pasa* is a hair ornament usually worn on one side of the head. It is commonly worn with the *tikka* (no. 154) and though used by brides, it is not exclusive to them. There is great variety in ornaments for the hair. Some, of disc shape, are worn on the braid; others (in the south) represent lunar or solar deities and are worn on either side of the head (see no. 50). Ornaments for the hair, however, imply that the occasion is extremely formal. Classical Indian dancers perhaps have the greatest use for them.

154
Hair ornament (tikka)
Gold, chased and pierced with red and white stones
E. Africa; 20th century
H 15 cm   L 5 cm; 20 grammes
Private collection

The *tikka* is a pendant on the forehead; its chain is fixed to the central parting of the hair. As the name implies, the *tikka* is a jewelled version of the red dot worn on the brow by Hindu women. A more elaborate version of the *tikka* would have jewelled bands, attached to the central pendant and encircling the head.

155
Earrings (lazark)
Gold, chased and pierced with red and white stones
E. Africa; 20th century
H 18 cm   L 3 cm; 30 grammes
Private collection

Heavy earrings sometimes have a chain attached, which is fixed either to the hair in a curve, or looped tautly over the ear, to ease the weight of the earring while preventing it from sagging in the lobe. The chain is called *lazark* or *martel* and is often embellished with small semi-precious stones like pearls or turquoises.

134 · The Darker Side of Gold

156
Choker (gulūband)
Gold, the solid stamped plaques decorated with cut-work and sheet-gold pendants
E. Africa; 20th century
H 4 cm L 23 cm; 67 grammes
Private collection

The *gulūband* usually has small linked squares, often set with gems. Older versions of the *gulūband* had a velvet backing for the greater comfort of the wearer.

159, 158
157

Twentieth-century Jewellery · 135

162 161 160
161 162 160

157 (opposite)
Bracelet (*gairah* or *gajral*)
Gold, the geometric plaques decorated with cut-work
E. Africa; 20th century
H 2.2 cm L 17 cm; 40 grammes
Private collection

Nos. 156-9 are part of a set. A *gairah* is a flexible bracelet of linked squares. Some *gairahs* are mounted on silk bands.

158 (opposite)
Earrings
Gold, the stamped plaques decorated with cut-work and sheet gold pendants
E. Africa; 20th century
H 6.8 cm L 1.8 cm; 6 grammes
Private collection

159 (opposite)
Ring (*angushtar* or *mundri*)
Gold, the stamped plaque decorated with cut-work with a faceted gold bead on either side
E. Africa; 20th century
DIAM. 1.9 cm H 2.2 cm; 5 grammes
Private collection

160
Pair of bracelets
Gold, the plain band decorated with twisted wire work
E. Africa; 20th century
DIAM. 5.6 cm H 1 cm; 80 grammes
Private collection

161
Pair of bracelets
Gold, the solid band decorated with an indented line at regular intervals
E. Africa; 20th century
DIAM. 6.2 cm; 40 grammes
Private collection

162
Pair of bracelets
Gold, the band decorated with a slightly raised floral pattern, alternating with incised gold half-beads
E. Africa; 20th century
DIAM. 6 cm; 40 grammes
Private collection

136 · The Darker Side of Gold

163
Bracelet (*paṭrī*)
Gold, with pierced and chased floral design, with a granulated effect set with red and white stones with faceted outer bands
E. Africa; 20th century
DIAM. 5.6 cm H 3.2 cm; 65 grammes
Private collection

A *paṭrī* or *chūṛ* is a broad flat bangle, studded with stones. This is a good example of an extremely traditional piece of jewellery that continues to be popular.

164
Bangle (*kaṛā*)
Gold, the heavy band slightly curved on either side
E. Africa; 20th century
DIAM. 7.5 cm H 0.3 cm; 65 grammes
Private collection

Based on the steel *kaṛā* worn by Sikh men and some Sikh women, this extraordinarily solid bangle testifies both to the owner's religion and his wealth. Male jewellery, though not as profuse as jewellery for women, still has an equally long tradition. Chains and signet rings are the most popular forms of jewellery for men today.

165
Baby bangles
Gold, the edges of the plain flat band chased and slightly rounded
Bradford, England; 1972
DIAM. 3.5 cm H 1 cm; 40 grammes
Private collection

Ostensibly for a baby boy, the very weight of the bangles makes them unsuitable for such tiny wrists, but like no. 151 they belong to the category of 'investment' jewellery.

166
Brooch
Gold, chased flat shield-shaped ornament, with a steel pin
E. Africa; 20th century
H 3.2 cm L 2.2 cm;
Private collection

The brooch would be pinned to the central folds of the turban.

165 164
166 167 168

167
Ring
Gold, the plain band with chased edges, the dark blue enamelled plaque decorated with gold
E. Africa; 20th century
DIAM. 2 cm H 1.9 cm; 25 grammes
Private collection

This heavy, plain ring is typical of male jewellery. The amount of gold used is surprisingly high, and is slightly more than the weight of three sovereigns.

168
Ashoka ring
Engraved gold
Mysore, Karnataka, South India; 20th century
H 2 cm L 1.9 cm; 3 grammes
Private collection

The design, commonly used on rings for men, gives this piece its name. It derives from the Buddhist dharmic wheel of law that the Emperor Ashoka used on all his inscriptions.

169
Necklace (mangal-sutra)
Gold, the very fine chain of minute spiral links set with black glass beads
Coorg, Karnataka, South India; 20th century
L 43 cm; 2 grammes
Private collection

The *mangal-sutra* or *kartha-mani*, is a symbol of marriage in western and southern India. After the husband's death, the *mangal-sutra* is removed immediately. Removing it during the husband's lifetime is supposed to invite all sorts of misfortune on the husband.

170
Chain
Gold, the links interspersed with pieces of decorative sheet gold
Coorg, Karnataka, South India; 20th century
L 69.5 cm
Private collection

A chain is probably the first piece of jewellery (along with a pair of earrings) to be acquired by an Indian girl. They come in a variety of styles and lengths, ranging from the rope chain to the wheat-grain chain to the circular linked chain. This particular chain was given to a sixteen-year-old South Indian youth, when he shot his first man-eating tiger, by a grateful village.

171
Ring
Gold, set with chrysoberyl
Mysore, Karnataka, South India, 20th century
Private collection

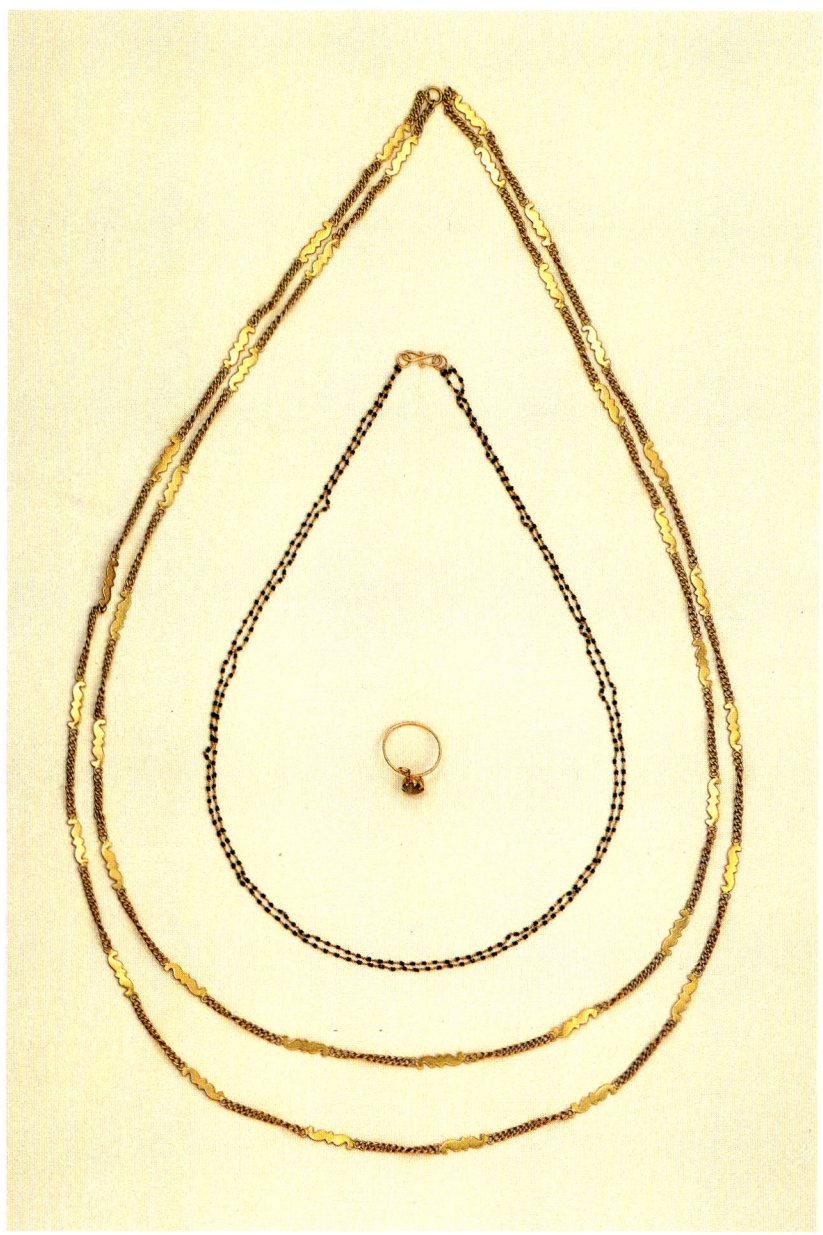

170
169
171

Glossary

aigrette: a jewelled ornament worn in the turban, often in the form of a feather.

Aphrodite: the Greek goddess of love, the Roman Venus.

bhagna: a goldsmith's blowpipe, usually made of bamboo.

Bodhisattva: a future Buddha who chooses, out of compassion for mankind, to postpone his (or her) ultimate liberation. They are portrayed wearing the finery, including jewellery, of the nobility and wealthy merchants.

cabochon: a polished stone with a smooth, curved surface.

cannetille: a style of gold filigree named after the French metal embroidery of the Napoleonic years made of fine twisted thread. On jewellery it takes the form of tightly-curled gold wires with trails of minute gold granules. In the West, it was fashionable in the 1820s, 1830s and 1840s, losing popularity by the middle of the century. In India, where the style was copied, it enjoyed favour for much longer.

champlevé: an enamelling technique where the metal is removed to make individual depressions into which the enamel is set. After firing, the enamel is polished down to the level of the surface of the object.

cornucopia: the horn of plenty in classical mythology; an emblem of abundance, pictured as a horn brimming with fruits, etc.

Gandhara: the ancient name for the region comprising parts of north-western Pakistan and of Afghanistan which was of great artistic, cultural and historical importance when Buddhism flourished there.

graha pravesh: no Hindu house in India will be occupied by the owners without this equivalent of a house warming, where the house is blessed by a priest and various rituals are conducted.

granulation: a technique of bonding minute spheres of gold to a gold surface, which reached its highest level of perfection under the Etruscans. It seems to have had a continuous history in India, unlike the West where the technique died out until revived in the mid-nineteenth century.

Gupta: a dynasty which ruled over northern India (320–c. 550 AD). During this time, ancient Indian civilisation arguably reached its highest point.

Hellenistic: from Hellas ('Greece'), referring to the Hellenistic period, which extended for several centuries from the death of Alexander in 323 BC, during which classical Greek civilisation spread far beyond Greece and its islands.

Iran: historically, this refers to the territories lying between present-day Afghanistan and Pakistan to the east, and Iraq and the Persian Gulf to the west.

Kushana: a dynasty of Central Asian origin which ruled over much of northern India in the 1st to 3rd centuries AD

jīgha: an ornament or jewel worn in the turban.

kalgī: a feather plume worn in the turban; the Persian word seems to have been used also to include the gold or gold and gem-set holder.

lac: a natural resin.

luted: from 'lute', a cement-like substance for coating joints.

makara: a mythical water beast.

mangal-sutra: comprises both the *thālī* and the black and gold beads on which it was strung.

megalithic grave: constructed from large slabs of stone. These graves are a feature of Iron Age cultures in the southern part of the Indian peninsula.

mina: enamel.

moniliform technique: a method of making gold beads by luting (see above) small gold balls together and bending them into a circle.

naga: snake. Snakes, or serpents, are said to guard the mineral wealth of the earth.

Naga: the Naga tribes live in north-eastern Assam; the origins of the name are unknown but it may mean 'naked people'.

Nilgiris: a hilly area in south India, notable for its temperate climate. Its Toda inhabitants are a group somewhat distinct from other peoples in south India.

Panjab: one of the provinces of both present-day India and Pakistan, historically it covered the area of the five rivers which give it its name (Persian *panj ab* = 5 waters).

***pavé*-set:** a method of covering, or 'paving,' the surface of an object with stones so that the stones touch each other, being held in place by grains of metal.

repoussé: (from the French 'thrust back') in relief, on thin metal beaten up from the reverse side.

sarpati: turban ornament, usually in three hinged parts, tied around the turban with silk threads.

sarpīch: originally used to describe any jewel placed in the front of a turban, held by bands of pearls, gemstones or gold beads which encircled the turban, it came specifically to mean a jewelled or enamelled aigrette.

Taxila: the most important city in Gandhara (see above) from c. 3rd century BC, situated near Islamabad. In extensive excavations, Sir John Marshall discovered the remains of at least three successive settlements, the most important being Sirkap (last half of 1st century BC to first half of 1st century AD.)

thālī: modern *thālīs* are small gold convex pendants studded with red and white stones, strung on black thread on a chain of black and gold beads. This symbolises marriage and has to be worn by the wife as long as the husband is alive. *Thālīs* may also be decorated with a pattern of gold rice grains.

yakshi: a female nature deity associated with trees and symbolising fertility.

Bibliography

Ahmad, Khwaja Muhammad, *Western Chalukyan Ornaments (Now Preserved in Hyderabad Museum)*, Hyderabad, 1359 Fasli/1949.

Allchin, Bridget and Raymond, *The Rise of Civilization in India and Pakistan*, Cambridge, 1982.

Anderson, J. Frank, *Riches of the Earth*, Windward, New York, 1981.

Arts of Bengal, The, see London: Whitechapel Art Gallery.

Ashton, Sir Leigh (ed.), *The Art of India and Pakistan*, exhibition catalogue, London, 1950.

Aziz, Abdul, *Arms and Jewellery of the Indian Mughuls*, Lahore, 1947.

Baden Powell, B.H., *A Hand-book of the Manufactures and Arts of the Punjab*, Lahore, 1872.

Balakrishnan, Param, 'The new gold rush', *Sunday*, vol. 15, no. 3 (13-19 December, 1987), pp. 22-9.

Barbier, Jean-Paul, *Art du Nagaland*, Geneva, 1982. Catalogue of an exhibition held at the Barbier-Muller Museum, Geneva, from 24 June 1982.

Becker, Vivienne, *Antique and 20th Century Jewellery*, London, 1980.

Becker, Vivienne and Munn, Geoffrey 'Robert Phillips. Underestimated Victorian Jeweller', *Antique Collector*, vol.10, 1983, pp.50-5.

Bhatia, Siddarth, 'Yellow clip security', *The Week*, vol. 5, no. 52 (13-19 December, 1987) pp. 38-41.
—— 'Global Sovereign', The Week, vol.5, no. 52 (13-19 December, 1987), p. 46.

Birdwood, George, *The Industrial Arts of India*, London, 1880.

Bivar, A.D.H., *Catalogue of the Western Asiatic Seals in the British Museum – Stamp Seals II: The Sassanian Dynasty*, London, 1969.

Brijbhushan, Jamila, *Indian Jewellery, Ornaments and Decorative Designs*, Bombay, 1955.
—— *Masterpieces of Indian Jewellery*, Bombay. 1979.

Brownrigg, Henry, 'The place of gold in Indian society', *Optima*, vol. 31, no. 1 (29 October 1982), pp. 18-29.

Brunel, Francis, *Jewellery of India. Five thousand years of tradition*, New Delhi, 1972.

Buchtal, H., 'The Haughton Collection of Gandhara Sculpture', *The Burlington Magazine*, LXXXVI, 1945, pp. 66-73.

Bury, Shirley, *Jewellery Gallery. Summary Catalogue*, Victoria & Albert Museum, London, 1982.

Casal, J-M and G., *Site Urbain et sites funeraires des environs de Pondichéry*, Paris, 1956.

Chandra, Rai Govind, *Studies in the development of ornaments and jewellery in Proto-historic India*, The Chowkhamba Sanskrit Studies vol. XLI, Varanasi, 1964.
—— *Indo-Greek Jewellery*, Abhinav Publications, New Delhi, 1979.

Chatterjee, K.N., 'The Use of Nose Ornaments in India', *Journal and Proceedings of the Asiatic Society of Bengal*, n.s. vol. XXIII, 1927, Calcutta, 1929, pp. 287-96.

Chetty, Ramanathan G.K., *Gems and Jewellery*, Madras (Kalakshetra Publications Press), 1980.

Czuma, Stanislas J., *Kushan Sculpture: Images from Early India*, exhibition catalogue, Cleveland, New York, Seattle, 1985-6.

Dalton, O.M., *Franks Bequest. Catalogue of the Finger Rings. Early Christian, Byzantine, Teutonic, Mediaeval and Later*, London, 1912

Dhavalikar, M.K., 'Classical Influence on Indian Coiffure and Jewellery', *Hind and Hellas*, Marg, vol. XXXVII, no. 2, Bombay.

Doshi, Saryu, 'Attire and Ornaments', *Shivaji and Facets of Maratha Culture*, Marg Publications, Bombay, 1982, pp. 166-72.
—— (ed.), *India and Greece, Connections and Parallels*, Marg Publications, Bombay, 1985.

Dubashi, Jayannath, 'Gold is still the most trusted asset' (an interview with gold-consultant Timothy Green), *Sunday*, vol.15, no.3 (13-19 December, 1987), p.24.

Filliozat, J. and Pattabiramin, P.Z., *Parures divines du Sud de l'Inde*, Publications de l'Institut Français d'Indologie, no.29, Pondicherry, 1966.

Finot, Louis, *Les lapidaires indiens*, Paris, 1896.

Flower, Margaret, *Victorian Jewellery*, London, 1967.

Foster, William, *Early Travels in India 1583-1619*, S.Chand & Co., Delhi, 1968 (reprint of 1921 Oxford edition).

— *The Embassy of Sir Thomas Roe to the Court of the Great Mogul 1615-1619*, Hakluyt Society, 1899; Kraus reprint, Nendeln/Liechtenstein, 1967.

Gere, Charlotte, *Victorian Jewellery Design*, London, 1972.

Gode, P.K., 'The Antiquity of the Hindoo Nose-Ornament called "Nath"', *Studies in Cultural History*, vol. II, Poona, 1960, pp. 142-60.

Hallade, Madeleine, *The Gandhara Style and the Evolution of Buddhist Art*, London, 1965.

Haque, Zulekha, *Gahana. Jewellery of Bangladesh*, Dhaka, 1984.

Havell, E.B., 'The Art Industries of the Madras Fresidency. I Jewellery', *JIAI*, vol. IV, April 1891, no. 34, pp. 7-8 and plates. Continued in vol. V no. 40, October 1892, pp. 29-34 and plates and vol. VI, October 1894, no. 48, pp. 70-1 and plates.

Hendley, T.H., 'Indian Jewellery', *The Journal of Indian Art and Industry*, vol. XII. A series of articles on the jewellery of India, from no. 95 (July 1906) to no. 107 (July 1909).
— *Memorials of the Jeypore Exhibition*, London, 1883 (3 vols.).

Higgins, Reynold, *Greek and Roman Jewellery*, 2nd ed., London, 1980

Hoffmann, Herbert and Davidson, Patricia F., *Greek Gold: Jewelry from the Age of Alexander*, exhibition catalogue (travelling exhibition first held in Brooklyn), Mainz, 1965.

Indian Heritage, The, see London: Victoria and Albert Museum.

Ivanov, A.A., Lukonin, V.G. and Smesova, L.S., *Oriental Jewellery from the Collection of the Special Treasury and State Hermitage Oriental Department*, Moscow, 1984.

Jacob, S.S. and Hendley, T.H., *Jeypore Enamels*, London, 1886.

Janata, Alfred, *Schmuck in Afghanistan*, Akademische Druck-v. Verlagsanstalt Graz, 1981.

Jenkins, Marilyn and Keene, Manuel, *Islamic Jewelry in the Metropolitan Museum of Art*, New York, 1982 (catalogue of an exhibition).

Jenkins, Marilyn, *Islamic Art in the Kuwait National Museum. The al-Sabah Collection*, London, 1983.

Krishnadasa, Rai, 'The Pink Enamelling of Banaras', *Chhavi: Golden Jubilee Volume*, Banaras, 1971, pp. 327-31.

Kunz, George Frederick, *The Curious Lore of Precious Stones*, Philadelphia, 1913; Dover Publications reprint, New York, 1971.

Lad, Gouri, 'Gems and jewelled articles: chronological and cultural dimensions with special reference to the Mahabharata', *Indica*, vol.16, no.2, September 1979, pp.191-9.

Latif, Momin, *Bijoux Moghols*, Brussels, 1982.

Lerner, Martin, *The Flame and the Lotus, Indian and Southeast Asian Art from The Kronos Collections*, The Metropolitan Museum of Art, New York, 1984

London: Victoria and Albert Museum, *The Indian Heritage*, London, 982.

London: Whitechapel Art Gallery, *Arts of Bengal*, London, 1980.

Longworth Dames, Mansell, *The Book of Duarte Barbosa*, Hakluyt Society, London, 1918, 2 vols.

Maclagan, E.D., *Monograph on the Gold and Silver Works of the Punjab 1888-9*, Lahore, 1890.

Markevitch, Elizabeth (ed.), *Indian Jewellery (Bijoux Indiens)*, Sotheby's (Switzerland), 1987.

Marshall, John, 'Buddhist Gold Jewellery' *Archaeological Survey of India. Annual Report 1902-3.*

Marshall, Sir John, *Taxila*, 3 vols, Cambridge, 1951.

Meen, V.B. and Tushingham, A.D., *Crown Jewels of Iran*, Toronto, 1968.

Midas [pseudonym], 'The Golden Ages', *The Week*, vol.5, no.52 (13-19 December, 1987), p.42.

Morley, Grace, 'On Applied Arts of India in Bharat Kala Bhavan; *Chhavi: Golden Jubilee Volume*, Banaras, 1971, pp. 107-29.

Mukharji, T.N., *Art Manufactures of India*, Glasgow, 1888.

Munn, Geoffrey C., *Castellani and Giuliano Revivalist Jewellers of the Nineteenth Century*, London, 1984.

Nadelhofer, Hans, *Cartier. Jewelers Extraordinary*, London, 1984.

O'Day, Deirdre, *Victorian Jewellery*, London, 1974.

Pal, M.K. and Roy Burman, B.K., *Jewellery and Ornaments in India – A Historical Outline*, Census of India 1971, series 1, paper no. 1, New Delhi, 1970.

Pal, Pratapaditya, *Indian Sculpture*, vol. I, Los Angeles, 1986.

Parmar, Swinder, 'The Six Wise Men', *The Week*, vol.5, no.52 (13-19 December, 1987), p.41.
—— 'The Golden Gangs', *The Week*, vol.5, no.52 (13-19 December, 1987), pp.43-5.

Pressmar, Emma, *Indische Ringe*, Frankfurt am Main, 1982.

Rogers, Alexander and Beveridge, Henry, *The Tūzūk-i-Jahāngīrī or Memoirs of Jahangir*, London, 1909 (vol.I), 1914 (vol.II).

Sahay, Sachidanand, *Indian Costume, Coiffure and Ornament*, New Delhi, 1975.

Sarianidi, Viktor, 'Die Schatze der Kuschanen-Könige', *Afghanistan Journal*, vol.6, pt.4, 1979, pp.121-32.

Sen, Jyoti and Das Gupta, Kumar, Pranab, *Ornaments in India. A Study in Culture Trait Distribution*, Anthropological Survey of India, Indian Museum, Calcutta, 1973.

Sharma, Vinod, 'Glittering Catches', *The Week*, vol.5, no.52 (13-19 December, 1987), pp. 44-5.

Spink, Michael (ed.), *Islamic Jewellery*, London, 1986.

Spink & Son Ltd, *Islamic and Hindu Jewellery*, London 1988.

Stronge, Susan, 'Mughal Jewellery', *Jewellery Studies*, vol. 1, 1983-4, London, pp. 49-53 and pls. IIB & III.
—— 'Jewels for the Mughal Court', *The V&A Album 5*, London, 1986, pp. 308-17.

Tagore, Sir Sourindro Mohun, *Maṇi Mālā or A Treatise on Gems*, Calcutta, 1879 (part I), 1881 (part II).

Tait, Hugh (ed.), *Seven Thousand Years of Jewellery*, London, (British Museum), 1986.

Tewari, S.P., *Nupura, The Anklet in Indian Literature and Art*, Delhi, 1982.

Untracht, Oppi, *Jewelry. Concepts and Technology*, Robert Hale Ltd., London, 1982.

Vinson, Julien, 'Les bijoux indiens du pays tamoul (Pondichéry)', *Journal asiatique*, mars-avril, 1904, x^{e}série, t.III, pp.239-57.

Welch, Stuart Cary et al., *The Emperor's Album: Images of Mughal India*, Metropolitan Museum of Art, New York, 1987.

Welch, Stuart Cary, *India. Art and Culture 1300-1900*, New York, 1985.

Wilkinson, Wynyard T., *Indian Colonial Silver European Silversmiths in India (1790-1860) and their Marks*, London, 1973.
—— *The Makers of Indian Colonial Silver. A Register of European Watchmakers and Clockmakers in India 1760-1860*, London, 1987.

Zwalf, W. (ed.), *Buddhism, Art and Faith*, London, 1985.

Index

Numbers in *italics* refer to catalogue entries

Abu'l Fazl, 29, 30
Afghanistan, *17*
Agra, 30, 33, *109*
Ahin Posh, *17*
A'in-i Akbari, 28, *90*
Ajanta, 13, *87*
Ajmir, *36*
Akbar, 27, fig. 5, 28, 29, 33, *76*
Akbarnama, fig. 5, fig. 7, 30, 33, *76*
Allard, General, *64*
ᶜAliverdi Khan, Nawab of Bengal 35, fig. 11, *37*
Amritsar, 47
amulet, *17*, 44, *62*
Ananta, *49*
animal style, 13
anklets, *105, 106, 107*
Aphrodite, *2*
Arabic, 41, *149*
armlets, 13, 15, 40, 48, 49, *78, 81, 82, 83, 84, 86, 90, 128*
Art Museum, Princeton University, *26*
Artemis, *26*
Arts and Crafts movement, 46
Asaf ad-Daula of Oudh, 37
Ashoka, *168*
Assam, 48, *126*
Athena, *26*
Audley End, Saffron Walden 41
Aurangzeb, 35

Babbu Singh, Benares enameller 37, *96*
Bactrian, 27
Bangalore, *49, 118*
Bangladesh, *46, 87, 145-50*
bangles, 12, *49, 88, 89, 91, 129, 164, 165*
Barbier, Jean-Paul, *49*
Barbosa, Duarte 27, 29
Baroda, 47, *107, 116*
beads, 13, *7, 8, 9, 74, 130, 131, 138, 139*
Benares (Varanasi), *53, 96*
Bengal, *32, 37, 78, 90, 96, 98, 99, 119, 136, 137*
Bernier, François, 27, 35
Bharat Kala Bhavan, *62*
Bhim Singh, Maharana of Mewar, fig. 12, 37, *38*
Bhudevi, *49*
Bihar, *18, 25*
Bijapur, 27, *118*
Bimaram reliquary, 11
Bodhgaya, *18, 25*

Bodhisattva, fig. 3, 13, *17*
Bombay, 44, 51, *87, 118, 134*
Boulton, Matthew, 54
bracelet, 15, *18, 78, 85, 119, 132-7, 7, 152, 157, 160-2, 163*
Bradford, England, *165*
Brahmi script, 28, 29, 30, 31
Brahmin, *117, 121*
British, 37, 41, 42, 44
British Museum, 11, *16-25, 27-36, 40, 41*
Brogden, John, 44, *122*
brooches, *23, 77, 114-6, 118, 120, 121, 101-103, 166*
Buddha, the, 13, *18, 25, 32*
Buddhist, *1*, 13, 15, *25, 32, 168*
Burges, William, 40, fig. 15, 41
Burhanpur (Brampore), 33
Burma, 48, *111*

Calcutta, 13, 44, 37, 55, 74, *105, 135-7*
Calicut, 27, *73, 75*
Cambay, 33
cannetille, 44, *118*
Cartier, fig. 19, 46, 47
Castellani, 40, *103, 122*
Central Banks of India, 11
chains, gold, 15, *25*, 44, *76, 152, 155, 170*
Chakravartin, 12
Chalukya, 35
Chandellas, 15
Chandragputa II, 30
Chester Beatty Library, Dublin, *62*
Chola bronzes, 15
Clarke, Caspar Purdon, 42, 46, *49, 70, 72*
claw settings, 30, 44, *98, 111, 116, 144*
Cleveland Museum of Art, *26*
Clive, George, 43, fig. 18
Clive, Lady, 43
Clive, Robert, 37, 42, *37*
cobra, *51, 58, 130, 131*
coins, 11, *14, 27-36*
Coorg, *130, 131, 132, 139, 169, 170, 171*
crucifix, *109*
Cunningham, Sir Alexander, *18, 29, 32*
Curzon, Lord, 79

Dalip Singh, *64*
Deccan, 35, 38
Delhi, 37, 47, *45, 47, 52, 83, 96, 118*
devanagari script, *34*, 40
Dhaka (Dacca), *145-50*
diadems, 13, *26*

Diaghilev, 46
dowry system, 11, 115, 116, *150*

ear ornaments, 20, 29, 40, *52, 53, 54, 56-9*
earrings, fig. 2, 12, 13, 15, *3, 4, 5, 6, 55, 130, 143-7, 155, 158*
East Africa, *151-4, 166, 167*
East India Company, 30, *143, 144, 108*
Eastern Chalukyan, 35
Eastlake, Sir Charles, 46
Egyptians, ancient, 11
Elliot family, *19*
Elliot, Sir Walter, *20, 21, 22, 23, 24, 25*
enamel, enamelling: 11, 30, 37-8, 47, 37-44, 52, 63, 65-68, 78, 79, 81, 82, 83, 93, 94, 96, 97, 109, 110, 134, 145, 149, 167; *basse taille*, 40; *champlevé*, 37; Benares, 37; Jaipur, 37, 47, 39, 40, 79, 80, 116; Lahore, 38, 64; Lucknow, 47; Murshidabad, 37; Sind, 96
enamellers, 30, 37
English, 44, *49*
Enlightenment Throne *18*
Etruscans, 30
Europe, European, 29, 33, 42, 43, 44, 47, 44, 53, 54, 78, 93, 98, 99, 109, 111-4, 116, 118, 119, 121, 122

Faizabad, fig. 6, 37, *94*
filigree, *53, 54, 55, 56, 73, 75*, 119, *133, 135*
forehead ornament, 44, 47, *48*
France, 54

Gandhara, fig. 3, 13, 15, *16, 17*
Ganesha, *122, 128*
Gangeyadeva, 33
Garuda, 28, *128, 130*
Gauda, 32
Gentil album, fig. 6, 29, 37, 44, *94*
George V, 47
gilding, gilt, 11, *1, 72*
girdle, 13, 15
Giuliano, Carlo, 44, *122*
Goa, 33
Gold: qualities: 11; sources, 11, 115; uses, 11; repoussé, 13, *1, 24, 26, 30, 42, 49, 51, 69, 77, 91, 122, 128, 130*; techniques, 30; inlaying, 30; engraving, 30, *93, 98, 99, 100, 105, 107, 111, 114, 131, 168*; chasing, 38, *119, 120, 121, 123, 128, 151-5, 163, 165, 167*; not worn on feet, 38, *107,*
123, 120; vogue in Europe, 47; use in Indian jewellery, 47; 'cut work', *54, 55, 88, 89, 133, 150, 156-9*; acquisition and cost of, 115, 120; India's absorption of, 115; and feminity, 116; caratage, 116, 117; weighing of, 117; hallmarking, 118; Gold Control Act, 1963, 119; use in Hindu ritual, 120-1; talismanic properties, 121; see also filigree, granulation
Goldsmiths, 15, 30, 43, 44, *116, 128*, 116, 117, 118, 119, 120
Granulation, fig. 2, 13, *3, 4, 5, 6, 20, 23, 30, 40, 57, 58, 71, 74, 75, 106, 118, 163*
Great Exhibition, London, 1851, 44, *73, 84, 85*
Greek, 13, *2, 3, 10, 12, 13, 14*
Gujranwala, 47
Gulbarga, 118
Gupta, 11, 13, 15, *6, 13, 28, 29, 30, 31*

Haidar ᶜAli of Mysore, 41
hair ornaments, *45, 46, 49, 51, 153, 154*
hairpin finials, 13, *2, 16*
Hamilton & Co, Calcutta, 44
Hanuman, *128*
Harappan, 11, 12
Hariti, 13, *1, 14, 26*
Hastings, Warren, 43
Hawkins, William, 27
Hellenistic, 13, *1, 2, 3, 13, 26*
Hercules, 13
Hermitage, the, 37
Hicky, William, 43
Hindu, Hindus, 28, 30, 38, 40, 41, 77, 119, 122, 128, 116, 120, 154
Hindustan, 29
Hoysala style, 15
Hunarmand, 33
Hunt, Holman, 46
huqqa, 37, 42
Hyderabad, Sind, 37

Indian Museum, 44, 46, 47, *56, 67, 68, 71, 83, 88, 96, 114*
Indore, 119, 120
Iran, Iranian, *10, 11, 14, 28, 29, 37, 46, 70, 95, 96*
Islamic, 46

Jaipur, *38-41*; treasury, 37, 47, *38, 41, 43*; see also enamel
Jagath Seth, 43, *108*
Jahangir, fig. 8, *36*, 30, 39, *109*

Jalalabad, 17
James I of England, 30, 33
Jammu, 143
Jamsetjee Jeejeebhoy School of Art, Bombay, 118
Jesuits, 33, 109
jīgha, 28, 35, 37, 38, 39, 40, 41, 42
Jones, Owen, 44

Kabul, 37, 96
Kaisar Agha, 37, 96
Kalachuri, 33
kalgī, 28
Kanarese (Kannada), 35, 100
Kanauj, 34
Kanishka I, 27
Kanpur, 133
Kapurthala, Maharaja of, fig. 19
Karnataka, 11, 116, 120, 121, 130, 131
Karttikeya, 31, 77
Kashmir, 143
Kautilya, 28
Khajuraho, 15
khil'at, 43
Khurram, Prince (later Shah Jahan), fig. 8, 30
Kohi-i-Noor, 44
Koran, Koranic, 62
Krishna, 119; see also Shrinathji
Krishnadasa, Rai, 37, 96
Kronos collections, fig. 1, 12
Kubera, 1
Kulu, 61
Kamaragupta I, 31
kundan, 30, 119
Kushana, fig. 3, 1, 13, 14, 26, 27
Kutch, 123
Kuwait National Museum, 93

Lahore, 37, 38, 64, 109, 144; see also enamelling
Lakshmi, 30, 33, 77, 128, 120, 121, 130, 131
Légion d'Honneur, 38, 64
Liberty, Arthur Lazenby, 44
lockets, 79
London, 43, 47, 57, 90, 92, 110
Lucknow, 37, 96, 119, 133; see also enamelling
Lulls, Arnold, fig. 9, 33

Madras, 22, 40, 42, figs. 16 and 17, 44, 48, 57, 91, 92, 106, 111-8, 122, 118
Madras Presidency, 38
Madura, 70
Mahabodhi temple, 18
makara, 13, 78, 91, 136
Malabar, 71
Malcolm, Sir John, 128
Malwa, 88, 89
Mangalore, 121
mangal-sutra, 119, 131, 169
marriage jewellery, 42, 69-71, 116, 118, 119, 130, 131, 132, 136, 151, 152, 169
Marwaris, 12
Mathura, 13
Metropolitan Museum of Art, fig. 1, 12, 93
mina, minakar, 30, 119; see also enamelling
Mir Ja'far ʿAli Khan, 37, 37
Mirzapur, 56
moniliform technique, 22
Mughals, 11, 36, 27-38 passim, 40, 37, 38, 40, 62, 63, 81, 82, 93, 97, 109, 110, 119
Muhammad Shah, Mughal emperor, 108
Mukarrab Khan, 33
Murshidabad, 35, fig. 11, 38, 37
Muslim, 28, 29, 30, 40, 49, 76, 133, 149
Mysore, 40, 41, 118, 138, 140-2, 168, 171

Nadelhofer, Hans, 46, 47
Nadir Shah of Iran, 37
naga, 40
Nagas, 48-49, 120-9
Naga Hills, 48
Nandi, 40, 69, 100-2
Nathdvara, 80, 86
Navaratna, 40, 82, 83, 146
necklaces, necklets, 13, 15, 27, 28, 42, 49, 65, 66, 67, 68-76, 78, 110, 114, 119, 124, 126, 130, 131, 138-40, 151, 156, 169
Nemean lion, 13
Nepal, 11
niello, 30, 128
Nilgiri Hills, 19, 20, 21, 22, 23, 24, 25
nose ring, 29-30, 60, 61

Orr, P, of Madras, 44, 46, 111, 122
Oudh, 37, 46, 90

Pala, 15
Panchika, 1
Panjab, 1, 2, 3, 4, 5, 6, 26, 47, 104, 132
Paris Exhibition, 1867, 44, 47, 56, 76, 83
Parks, Mrs Fanny, 44, 46, 76
Partabgarh, 44, 119, 120
Parvati, 69, 120
Patiala, 47
pendants, 21, 40, 62, 63, 80, 114, 117, 124
Peshawar, 47
Persian language, 36, 41, 95, 108
Phillips, Robert, 44, 94, 109
Plassey, Battle of, 37
Pliny the Elder, 115
Poiret, Paul, 46
Pondicherry, 22
Portuguese, 33
Prince of Wales, Indian tour 1875, 42, 77, 121, 122
Pushkar, fig. 25

Rajaraja, Eastern Chalukyan king, 35
Rama, 34, 128
Ranjit Singh, 38, 47, 64
Rashtrakuta dynasty, 34
reliquaries, 11, 13, 1, 15
Renaissance jewellery, 33, 93
Reynolds, Joshua, fig. 18, 49
rings, 11, 27, 96, 97, 98, 99, 100, 101, 103, 111-3, 152, 159, 167, 168, 171; thumb rings, 27, 93, 94; seal rings, 95, 108; Nandi rings, 101, 102; mirror ring, 104
Roe, Sir Thomas, 27, 30, 33
Roman, 1, 2, 10, 12, 14
Rossetti, Dante Gabriel, 46, 91
rudraksha bead, 38, 91
Ruskin, John, 44
Russia, 13, 37
Rutlam, 119-21

Sa'di, 95
Samarkhand, 27
Samudragupta I, 28
Sanskrit, 15, 29, 70, 83
Sarasvati, 122
Sarmatian jewellery, 13
sarpīch, 28, 35
Schwaiger, Imre, 47
Scindia, Maharani of, 76
Scythian jewellery, 13
seals, 10, 11, 12, 13, 14, 35, 95, 108
Seringapatam, 40
serpents, 49, 121; see also cobras
Shah ʿAlam Bahadur Shah, 35
Shah Jahan, 33, 35, fig. 10, 62, 93; see also Khurram, Prince
Shah Rukh of Samarkhand, 27
Shashanka, 32
Shiva, 27, 32, 38, 40, 69, 91, 100, 101, 122
shoes, 123
Shore, Sir John, 43, 108
Shridevi, 49
Shrinathji, 80, 86
Sikh, 164, 166
Sind, 96
Siraj ad-Daula, 35, 37, 37
Sirkap, 3
South Africa, 115
South Kensington Museum, 44, 46, 49, 76, 90; see also Victoria and Albert Musuem
Subrahmanya, 76
Surat, 33
Surya, 49
swami work, 42, 46, 122
Swat, 15

Tagore, Rabindranath, 122
Tagore, Surendranath, 40
Talpurs of Sind, 37, 96
Tamilnadu, 13, 22, 25, fig. 24, 42, 59, 69
Tamluk (Tamralipti), fig. 1, 13
Tanjore (Thanjavur), 38, fig. 13, fig. 14, 42, 43, 92
Ta'vīz, 62
Taxila, 13, 1, 2, 3, 4, 15, 16, 19, 26
Telegu, 35
thālī, 118, 119, 69-71
Tibet, 11
tiger claws, 76, 77
Timur, 35
Tipu Sultan of Mysore, 40, 41
Tirupathi, 121
Toussaint, Jeanne, 47
Travancore, 71, 77
Treasury, Mughal, 27, 28, 35, 38
Tripuri, 33
Trivandrum, 29
turban jewels, 27, 8, 33-37, 43, 46, 37-43; see also kalgī, jīgha, sarpīch

Udaipur, fig. 12, 42

Varanasi, see Benares
Varthema, Ludovico de, 27
Vedic gods, 11
Vellore, 58, 72
Vengi, 35
Venus, 2
Victoria, Queen, 46
Victoria and Albert Museum, 37, 38, 62, 91, 92, 93; see also South Kensington Museum
Victorian jewellery, 30, 78, 85
Vijayanagar, 27, 29
Vishnu, fig. 4, 28, 35, 49, 86, 119, 122, 128

Watherston and Brogden, 44
Watson, Admiral Charles, 37, 43, 37, 81, 109
Wilkinson, Wynyard, 43, 44

yakshi, fig. 1, 13

Zaveri family of jewellers, 118-9
zodaic, 40